MOUSEMOBILE

ALSO BY PRUDENCE BREITROSE

Mousenet

MOUSEMOBILE

by prudence breitrose

illustrated by stephanie yue

Disney•HYPERION BOOKS

NEW YORK

Printed in the United States of America
First Edition

1 3 5 7 9 10 8 6 4 2

G475-5664-5-13213

Library of Congress Cataloging-in-Publication Data
Breitrose, Prudence E.
Mousemobile / by Prudence Breitrose ;
illustrations by Stephanie Yue.—First edition.
pages cm.—(A Mousenet book)
Summary: "Eleven-year-old Megan and her cousin Joey have a summer job working
with computer-savvy mice to spread the word about climate change. But when there's
trouble at Headquarters, Megan and Joey find themselves on a cross-country journey to
save Mouse Nation, and the planet, from a mysterious enemy"—Provided by publisher.
ISBN 978-1-4231-7412-7 (hardback)—ISBN 1-4231-7412-7
[1. Mice—Fiction. 2. Global warming—Fiction. 3. Computers—Fiction.
4. Inventions—Fiction. 5. Cousins—Fiction. 6. Voyages and travels—Fiction.]
I. Yue, Stephanie, illustrator. II. Title.
PZ7.B84895Mn 2013
[Fic]—dc23   2013020527

Reinforced binding

Visit www.disneyhyperionbooks.com

SUSTAINABLE FORESTRY INITIATIVE   Certified Sourcing
www.sfiprogram.org
SFI-00993

THIS LABEL APPLIES TO TEXT STOCK

For all those humans who work valiantly,
like these mice, to prevent climate change.

chapter one

B arf," said the mouse on Megan's shoulder, as she opened the door of her uncle's house.

Yes, it smelled bad. Last night Uncle Fred had said, "I'll take out the trash in the morning," but he must have forgotten, and an extra day in this Cleveland summer, in a house where the air-conditioning was usually turned off for the sake of the planet, was way too much for it.

And trash was not the only problem.

Uncle Fred must have been distracted at breakfast time, maybe thinking about a new invention, because he'd left eggshells festooned with waffle mix on the table, while bacon grease had spilled onto the magazine he'd been reading.

Megan's *mom* would never have made such a mess. In fact, she'd have left something special on the kitchen table, *something* to celebrate the fact that Megan had just finished the computer course she'd been taking. At least a special cookie or a note or a flower from Uncle Fred's overgrown yard.

Something better than eggshells and bacon grease and bits of waffle, all scented with the odor of trash can.

Megan checked her phone to see if there might at least be a message from her mom: but no, of course not. Not till Sunday. That was the only day of the week her mom could call or e-mail from the summer camp where she was working, off in the Rocky Mountains. Two days to wait.

"What was it your mom said?" asked Trey from her shoulder, surveying the mess. He made his voice higher. "'My little brother can't even look after himself, let alone *you!*'"

That's *exactly* what her mom had said when she'd taken off for the Rockies. She wanted Megan to go stay with her dad in Oregon. She'd be going there anyway, wouldn't she, at the end of the summer, so why not a few weeks early? And wouldn't Oregon be just great—so cool and green after the steamy heat of Cleveland?

Well yes, Megan loved Oregon. She had nothing against Oregon, or her dad, or her stepmother, Annie. But, as she told her mom, she really had to stay in Cleveland.

"Whatever for?" her mom had asked.

Megan wasn't allowed to tell her mom the truth about mice, so she had gone a bit red. "Well, there's my job . . ."

Her mom had hooted with laughter because (as she pointed out) at eleven you're not exactly old enough for a *real* job. Puttering around in her uncle's office, was that really so important?

Luckily, as it turned out, Megan *had* to stay in Cleveland for the next few weeks at least: her dad and Annie weren't home. They were taking a cruise to Alaska, followed by some time in British Columbia checking out green restaurants just like the one they owned in Oregon. And they wouldn't be back until it was almost time for Megan to join them.

So she was still here, which was great, because for the only four Humans Who Knew that mice had evolved, Cleveland was where the action was. True, on hot days, the forests of Oregon beckoned, and in some ways Megan couldn't wait to get there—especially if her step-cousin, Joey, came along too with his dad, Jake, who could take them hiking and white-water rafting and fishing and hunting for shells on the beach.

But with or without Joey and Jake, Oregon was a few weeks away. For now, Megan had the pleasure of the heat and her uncle's kitchen. She was still gazing at the mess and wondering where to start when Joey arrived.

"Phew," he said, wrinkling his nose. "Pee-you. Megan, your uncle . . ."

"I know, I know, I know," she said, scowling at him because *she* was the only person in the world who was allowed to speak neck, which did nothing to cool either of them down. "All the more reason for you guys to fix it."

"Yeah, fix it, Trey," said Joey. "What's taking so long?"

"Hey, we're only mice," sad Trey. "Not miracle workers."

If it hadn't been so hot, Megan might have argued about the miracle bit, because ever since Trey had approached her in the night last year—ever since she'd become the first human in the history of the world to know the truth about mice—there had been one miracle after another. Like the series of spells the mice had arranged to manipulate Joey, in Operation Mouse Magic (with Kindness). Spells to help Joey's dad do well at his job, spells to fix his grandma's leaky roof, and spells to find his lost cat at the speed of light.

It was never real magic, of course. As Trey often said, "You don't need magic when you have mice." But if mice had managed to arrange all those good deeds, couldn't they please move a bit faster on cooling the planet?

"Have patience," said Trey. "It'll take a year or two."

They'd made a good start, through Operation Cool It. Mice with tiny Thumbtop computers had already persuaded at least two senators to change their votes on important climate bills. At least one famous radio guy had stopped saying climate change was a hoax. And there were signs that just plain folks in America were starting to save energy because of all the helpful hints that popped up in front of them, thanks to their resident mice.

In fact, Cool It was becoming so successful that a billionaire who made his money from oil and coal was offering rewards for information about the mysterious organization that was cutting into his profits.

But that didn't do much to help cool down the Cleveland streets right now. Megan and Joey were glad to reach their destination, which looked like an ordinary house except for the sign in front that said:

Planet Mouse
Home of the Thumbtop
and the Blob
Made in Cleveland by Mice

Which was okay to say, because who'd ever believe it?

In the office, the air-conditioning was set fairly high for the sake of the planet, but it was still much cooler than the street. And a fan was helping out, with three mice parked in front of it, their ears and whiskers blown back by the wind.

Megan and Joey knelt down beside the mice, who turned to greet them. Julia headed for Megan's shoulder and leaned against her neck, while Curly and Larry made a beeline for Joey. Curly had been his special friend ever since Joey had held him captive for a short time last year. And Larry . . . well, Larry was a mouse who could bore you to tears on the subject of almost any sport you could name, and right now he was focusing all his attention on Joey and his team of Little League all-stars.

"Yo," said Jake, who was lounging behind the desk, looking cool, as always. "All done with summer school? Both of you official computer geeks? Ready to help the Cool It team with their algorithms?"

"I wish," said Megan, because there was no way. The mice who ran Cool It had spent years watching human nerds in the great computer companies of Silicon Valley, and were truly amazing at writing computer programs. No way a kid could catch up after one summer course.

"How do you like this heat?" asked Jake. "Can't wait to get to Oregon? Me too."

"But you might not be coming, right?" said Megan. "If Joey's team keeps winning. If he goes all the way to the State Championship and the Regionals and the World Series, then you'll both have to go to Pennsylvania or wherever."

"Don't say it, don't say it, don't say it," said Joey, leaping up and dancing around the room with his hands over his ears, deeply superstitious about what might happen if you predicted victory. "No way we're that good. Oregon, here we come."

Curly couldn't take that, because mice never predict defeat. He jumped onto the desk so he could look Joey in the face as he tapped his head with his left paw, meaning "Think" in the silent language used by all but a handful of mice. Then he thrust his right paw into the air. The sign for "Positive."

"Okay, I should think positive," said Joey, smiling down at him.

Then Larry took the conversation one step further and launched into a long series of signs that none of the humans recognized.

"Trey!" said Megan. "Help!"

Trey wasn't really into baseball, but when you're one of the very few mice who have been trained to talk, it's your job to translate.

"Larry thinks Joey's team *can* win the State Championship, then the Regionals, and then the World Series, but only if they shake things up a bit, like have Joey bat cleanup, put Chad at shortstop, try Frankie in right field—really, you don't want to know."

Megan reached out to stroke Larry, to show that she loved him even if he was the most boring sports nut in the world.

"Do you want us to help?" Trey asked. "Like make sure Joey's team gets to the World Series? Or make sure it doesn't?"

"No way!" shouted Jake and Joey together, laughing.

"Oops," Trey said. "Only asking. But don't worry, we'll leave it all up to you and your slider, or whatever you call it. Paws off."

Megan laughed with the others, but she couldn't help being a bit conflicted on the issue of Joey's team winning or losing. On the one hand, of course it would be so great if Joey went all the way to the Little League World Series in Pennsylvania. Who couldn't want that? But the alternative would be great too, wouldn't it? The three of them going to Oregon? Especially if they drove there by way of her mom's camp, which was something Jake had suggested.

To see her mom in *that* place, with *those* people? Wouldn't that be one of the best things ever?

chapter two

It was in one of their regular videoconferences, at the beginning of summer, that the Big Cheese, leader of the Mouse Nation, had announced his plans for sending Megan's mom away.

The humans had put the Susie Miller question on the agenda, as they had done several times before. Could they please tell her the truth, finally? Because Susie had no clue about mice. And when your mom, or your sister, or your friend doesn't know the most important thing about you—doesn't know the biggest secret in the history of the world—that can be a problem.

It was Megan who'd made the pitch one more time, because she was the only human who'd ever met the Big Cheese, and she felt there was a bond.

"It's really hard for kids to keep secrets from their mothers," she had said. "For one thing, human mothers are very good at guessing when you aren't telling the truth. And my mom's getting suspicious."

It was true. Like the time her mom had come into her bedroom, bare feet making no sound, while Trey was in the middle of a sentence. Megan had quickly switched to a Trey-voice, the way a six-year-old might pretend her doll was talking: "I am a mousie and I want my mousie dinner!"

Which got her a very strange look from her mom.

"I am aware of the impediments in your parental situation," said the Big Cheese. His signs were being translated by Talking Mouse Five, who called himself Sir Quentin—a mouse who had learned to talk with the help of old British historical dramas. And he never used a short word if a long one would do. This sometimes drove Megan and Joey nuts even though, as Jake said, it was good for them because by the time they had to face the SAT in high school, they'd know ten times as many long words as anyone else.

Sir Quentin continued his interpretation: "I am cognizant of your parent's propensity to prioritize her promulgations with a preference for verity, for which I believe the following anecdote will be illustrative."

That was way too many syllables even for Jake, so he turned

down the sound and let Trey interpret the Big Cheese's signs.

"The boss is worried because Megan's mom is way too truthful," Trey whispered. "We had a guy eavesdropping at Cleveland State when she was teaching there, and a friend asked what she thought of her new dress. Your mom told her it made her look kind of fat, which didn't go down at all well."

Megan smiled. That was so like her mom. She hardly ever shaved corners off the truth.

"Until such time as she can suppress this tendency to tell the truth," the Big Cheese continued, "I cannot take the risk of telling her our secret, a secret that you will agree is of planetary importance. However . . ."

He paused for effect, and there was a gleam in his eye. "However," he continued, "I have found a temporary solution to your problem. Indeed, I have devised an excellent plan that will kill two cats with one stone."

"It's birds," Joey said. "Kill two *birds* with one stone."

The Big Cheese gave the webcam one of those whisker-shriveling looks that all mice (and a few humans) dread.

"I am well aware of your metaphor," he said. "But we have no quarrel with birds, nor a wish to kill them, with the possible exception of hawks and owls. My plan should achieve the following objectives: First, it will remove the parent from

Cleveland, so there will be less danger that she might stumble upon our secret. Second, it will test her ability to keep important information to herself. Finally, it will place her where she can use her considerable talents for the benefit of the planet."

"Wow," said Uncle Fred. "That's three cats, by my reckoning. What sort of job is it? Tracking polar bears? Checking up on penguins? Back in Australia with those—"

The Big Cheese held up his paw in the universal sign for "Stop."

"Trust us," was all he'd say. "Have faith. To say more might be to risk spilling the crackers."

"Shouldn't that be *beans*?" Joey asked. "Spilling the *beans*?"

"The bean," said the Big Cheese sternly, "plays havoc with the mouse digestive tract. We prefer crackers in our metaphors, as in our diet."

And it happened, a few days later.

Megan was in her room when she heard a great whoop of astonishment and delight. She ran downstairs to find her mom walking from one side of the kitchen to the other, running her hand through her springy fair hair. From time to time she stopped to gaze at the laptop on the kitchen table, as if it took a great many gazes to convince herself that the words were really there.

"I can't believe it! I just can't believe it! Someone sent my resume to . . . Oh, read it yourself," she commanded.

Megan looked quickly at the sender of the e-mail, and no, it hadn't come from anyone at mousenet.org—the e-mail address of the Mouse Nation. This was from a real human in a real foundation that did real work to stop climate change, and it said:

> We apologize for the short notice, but a
> comprehensive search has shown that you are
> the best candidate for the position we would like
> to offer you.

And it went on to ask Megan's mom to please come to a remote valley in the Rocky Mountains because:

> Our foundation has established a "summer camp"
> for movie stars. Perhaps more than any others
> in our society, such people have easy access to
> the media. And many are deeply concerned with
> environmental problems, including that of climate
> change. At Camp Green Stars, scientists like
> yourself will provide the necessary training so that

when the stars talk in public—or are interviewed
by reporters—they will know how to lead the
conversation around to climate change. And they
will know how to present the facts in the way that
best educates their "fans."

"Wow," said Megan, marveling at the power of mice. It was
indeed a perfect solution, a three-cat solution if ever there was
one. "When do you start?"

"They want me there in two days," said her mom. "That's

way too soon. I'll ask if I can put it off for a bit."

"Put it off?" Megan asked, her voice squeaky with surprise. Because why? When mice had come up with the dream job for her mom? The best job ever?

Her mom gave her a hug. "I just hate to leave in rush, without saying good-bye to everyone properly."

Which was odd because Susie Miller had gone off to work in Australia for months and months last year on a moment's notice, without a peep.

Uncle Fred had arrived home for dinner with Joey, who was staying with them while Jake was away in Chicago showing off his solar blobs at a trade show.

"Tell Uncle Fred about that e-mail, Mom," said Megan. "And tell *him* you want to put it off."

"Put it off?" exclaimed Uncle Fred, skimming through the e-mail. "Are you nuts?"

Then he gave Susie a bear hug, the sort of hug that's an excuse for whispering something.

Megan glanced at Joey, who shrugged. No clue. She was about to come right out and ask what the whispering had been about when Jake called, and her mom took the phone outside.

"I asked him to keep an eye on Megan until she goes to Oregon," she said when she came back in. "Make sure she eats properly and does her homework for summer school. No offense, Fred, but he's better at that sort of thing than you are."

"No offense," said Uncle Fred, and grinned to show he meant it.

Jake must have persuaded Susie to grab that job NOW, because she left for Camp Green Stars the next day.

When Megan had asked Trey how the mice had set up her mom's job, he'd said, "It really wasn't that hard. Same old same old, really. The billionaire who runs that foundation? We had guys feeding him visions of Green Stars in so many ways that he couldn't resist. We even used his grandkids. Of course he thought it was all his own idea. They always do, don't they? Then it was easy to send him a copy of your mom's resume."

Megan had smiled. She never ceased to marvel at the way mice could manipulate humans once they put their minds to it—whether it was something as simple as persuading people to turn off the lights, or as complicated as setting up camps for movie stars in the Rocky Mountains.

chapter three

egan missed her mom. Who wouldn't, when without her, Uncle Fred's house felt as if it were about to self-destruct under the weight of unwashed dishes? But in other ways it was a relief to have her gone. So good to live among mice and humans who had no secrets from each other.

And for a couple of weeks everything seemed to be going as well as could be expected on all fronts, as Joey won some more Little League games. And the business of Planet Mouse thrived. These successes even wrung a quote out of Trey:

"'All is for the best in the best of all possible worlds.' A French dude said that. Voltaire. Though I'm not sure he really meant it. Might have been sarcastic."

"Well, you mean it, don't you?" asked Megan.

"I guess," said Trey.

Because what could possibly go wrong?

Well, when exactly *did* things start to go wrong? What was the first ripple of trouble on the smooth surface of that summer? Could it have been the memo that whizzed through the mouse world one Wednesday afternoon?

It looked so harmless at the time, barely worth a giggle from Trey (who'd taken giggling for extra credit at the Talking Academy).

The Humans Who Knew were eating dinner at the house Jake had rented, a block from Uncle Fred's. As usual, their four main mice had been cruising the table for leftovers, when Trey slapped his head with a paw as if he'd suddenly noticed something.

"Julia!" he ordered, with his best giggle. "Put down that pie crust. It's human food. Didn't you get the memo?"

Julia made the "Laughing out loud" sign (paw to mouth, three quick pats) and went on eating.

"What memo?" asked Jake.

"Came in from the Big Cheese this afternoon," said Trey. "Hook up a Thumbtop and I'll show you."

Uncle Fred linked a Thumbtop to Jake's big computer so they could all read the e-mail that Trey showed them:

From: Topmouse@mousenet.org
To: All mice
Subject: Our Mouseness

Memo

Certain mice appear to have been led by our proximity to the larger species to crave human luxuries. Please be aware that any tendency to follow human customs or adopt human comforts will NOT BE TOLERATED. Any mouse found in violation of this order will be exiled.

As I have frequently stated, we are MICE, and must remain so in our habitats, our diets, and our social structure. Any progress must be made within the boundaries of an orderly evolution as decreed by your leaders.

"Wow," said Uncle Fred. "What brought that on?"

"I don't know," said Trey. "But I have my suspicions. There's a new mouse in town."

Still connected to the big monitor, he clicked his way to MouseTube, the site where mice park their videos, and wrote

"Savannah" in the search box. Up came a clip showing a mouse with a pink bow pasted to her head, the sort that humans stick on gift packages. The mouse rose to her hind feet and walked slowly toward the camera, her tail swishing gracefully from side to side.

When she got so close that her nose looked huge, she purred, "Hey there, world, anyone got a job out there for little Savannah? See, I'm stuck here at Headquarters, and it's not the greatest fit for a mouse who appreciates the finer things in life."

"Yikes!" said Joey. "I thought all you talking mice came out so serious. . . ."

"Not one of our greatest successes," said Trey. "That's what the head of the Talking Academy told me. Now he thinks it was a mistake letting her watch nothing but chick flicks, like *Beach Blondes* and *Hollywood Blondes*. She came out wanting slinky gowns and fast cars. Not a recipe for happiness if you're a mouse."

"Especially a mouse at Headquarters, I'd imagine," said Uncle Fred. "Pretty bleak there, isn't it? So this memo . . . ?"

"Whatever brought it on," Trey said, "it could well be something she did. I hope it doesn't get her into trouble, because she's not a bad mouse, deep down. I'll e-mail some friends. See what's going on."

But (as he told Megan much later) he found himself putting it off. No rush. And besides, he had a hunch he wouldn't like what he found—especially if it was something that made one talking mouse look ridiculous, and by extension all of them.

The Friday after the memo seemed as smooth as any, except that the Cleveland temperature soared, with humidity to match. Megan and Joey went early to their jobs in the factory at Planet Mouse because it was blessedly cool: even if humans could get by without much air-conditioning, the humming machinery and its workers could not.

Here, hundreds of mice toiled at assembly lines to make Thumbtops for the Mouse Nation, and solar blobs in the form of jewelry, or belt buckles, or eyeglass frames. Whatever would sell best to humans, and pay the expenses for the whole enterprise.

The assembly lines took up most of the floor space in what had once been a three-car garage, but there was still room for a workbench, where Uncle Fred was standing, looking huge compared to the hundreds of mice working on the factory floor. But then, he *was* huge, even bigger—around the middle, anyway—than when he'd been an All-American football player at Ohio State.

"I know what you're thinking," he said as Megan and Joey came in. "That I'm only in here for the cool. But I've actually been inventing something. Meet Thumbtop Two. Ta-da!"

He held out a tiny computer in his massive paw.

"It looks just like the others," said Megan.

"Ah-ha!" said her uncle. "That's the joy of it. Lots of new features in the same sleek package. It can shoot great video. And wait, there's more!"

He did the slow pirouette that mice use to show they're happy about something; though when Uncle Fred did pirouettes, he looked more like a cheerful elephant than a mouse. "I've tucked a telephone inside! I already e-mailed the Big Cheese about it, and he's all excited."

"A phone?" said Joey, with the half smile that often came to him when Megan's uncle was being particularly goofy.

"I know, I know," said Uncle Fred. "Not much use to mice when there's still only seven or eight who can talk. But maybe Trey here will have a sudden urge to chat with his friend Sir Quentin."

ill of Uncle Fred. Ever. "It stinks. So will you please help me clean it up?"

"What, woman's work?" said Joey, and even though Megan knew he was just trying to annoy her, she threw a piece of dried-up waffle at him, which was rash because he was eight months older than she was, and two inches taller, and the star pitcher on his Little League team. So if he'd chosen to hurl the waffle back, it might have done permanent damage.

If the house had felt hot, the street was worse. After Megan and Joey cleaned up most of the kitchen, they had to walk two blocks to their summer jobs, and the air tasted like the exhaust of a giant bus belching super-heated gasses into their faces.

"This has to be the hottest summer ever," said Megan, tugging on her soggy T-shirt to unglue it from her back.

"You think *you're* hot," said Trey, on her shoulder. "Try it if you can't sweat and you can't take your coat off. No zipper."

"Poor old Trey." Megan reached up to stroke him while he leaned against her

Trey chuckled. "Yeah, right," he said. "Good old Sir Q, with a—what?—a telephonic apparatus for transcontinental communication? I'd never get a word in."

"Or Savannah? Bet she'd like you to call her!" said Uncle Fred.

"Er . . ." Trey began.

"Then, when you guys aren't hogging the phone," Uncle Fred went on, "the Big Cheese can use it to text. Maybe he's up for that. And who knows, we might even sell them to humans!"

"For the person who has everything?" said Joey, not sounding very convinced. "For only—how much—a hundred bucks?"

"Whoa," said Uncle Fred. "I wouldn't charge a penny more than ninety-nine ninety-nine. Such a deal."

As Megan knew, her uncle was still a bit disappointed that not many humans wanted to buy the first generation of Thumbtops. Of course, as mice often said, it worked better for mice than for humans. Paws yes, fingers no. But as a cool gift? A full-fledged computer dangling from a key ring, even if you did need a magnifying glass to read the screen and a toothpick to pick out the right keys?

. . . .

When Uncle Fred had taken a last breath of cool factory air and headed back to the house, Megan set down the cage that Curly, Larry, and Julia rode in whenever they visited the factory. As everyone knew, the bars on the old birdcage were too far apart to actually imprison mice, so the three could come and go as they pleased. But the cage gave them a feeling of security, as if they were afraid that some foreman, or foremouse, might put them on the assembly line if they set a paw outside.

Megan couldn't blame them for wanting to avoid the assembly line. Who wouldn't? Mice spent four hours at a time on the line, for two shifts a day, going through the same motion again and again and again, whether it was pushing or pulling or yanking or lifting, their paws wrapped in tiny plastic mouse-gloves that the humans had made for them, while the rest of their bodies were encased in plastic sandwich bags to keep all vestiges of mouse dust out of the product.

The amazing thing was that the mice on the line didn't seem to mind. Whenever Uncle Fred and Jake needed a new batch of volunteers, they were overwhelmed by applications from mice all over northern Ohio. Sometimes as many as ten mice tried out for each job, and the guys who didn't make the cut—who didn't have the paw-eye coordination needed—were devastated.

. . . .

Megan loved her time in the factory. Light from the high windows glinted off the plastic coverings of the workers, who looked like the chorus of a mouse ballet moving to the rhythm of the assembly line as it took in all the tiny parts at one end, and spat out shiny new Thumbtops at the other.

She and Joey took turns doing what was needed to keep the labor force clean, healthy, and happy. On this particular Friday, it was Joey's turn for mousekeeping—cleaning up the workers' living quarters and refilling bowls with food and water. He would also empty and refill the trays of kitty litter—making sure that the picture of a cat on the front of the bag was turned away from any watching mice, because the sight of a cat can constipate a mouse, big time.

Megan's job today was her favorite: caring for the inner mouse. Making sure the workers were happy in their time off. She picked her way to the back of the garage, where a row of Thumbtops had been set up for the mice to surf on, including one with a sign reading:

SUGGESTIONS PLEASE

When suggestions had first started coming in, Megan had expected that some mice, at least, would be critical of the factory, or Headquarters, or the Big Cheese. That *someone* would rebel and tell the humans what they could do with their blankety-blank assembly line.

But today, as usual, the suggestions were bland in the extreme. Like this one:

Please, could we have a Sudoku tournament?

And:

Our chorus has been rehearsing. Could you help us arrange a concert?

Then came a suggestion that was truly a surprise, even from a mouse:

How about speeding up the assembly lines? Might be fun to see if we can go faster.

"Wow!" whispered Megan. "Is this guy for real? Or is he being sarcastic?"

"You ever meet a sarcastic mouse?" asked Trey, holding tightly to Megan's braid, as if he, too, might be hustled into a sandwich bag if he let go.

"Well, would *you* write something like that?" she asked. "Begging to work harder?"

"Me? Before I met you, sure. It's the way we're raised. One for all and all for mice. Like they tell us in our civics class—everything for the good of the nation, yada yada yada, not the individual mouse. That sort of thing."

"And now?"

Trey was thoughtful. "I wouldn't exactly *beg* to work harder. I guess some of the way humans think *has* rubbed off on me. Like not being crazy about the idea of living in a sandwich bag and working my tail off."

"I won't tell anyone," said Megan, reaching up to give him a little rub behind the ears.

Next she clicked on the folder for movie suggestions. Three mice wanted *An American Tail*. Again. Ten opted for *G-Force*. But the clear winner was *Ratatouille*, with twenty-five requests, because mice adore that movie and can sit through it a hundred times, even if the hero is a rat rather than a mouse. Megan loaded *Ratatouille* into the DVD player, leaving the remote where a mouse could easily jump on the PLAY button.

Her last job was to collect the output figures for the day from the production manager. She could understand most of his signs, thanks to the lessons in MSL that Julia gave her every day. But now Trey translated, just to make sure. Fifty thousand Thumbtops finished, to be sent out to mice. Two hundred boxes of assorted solar blobs to be shipped to humans. In other words, just a normal day at the factory.

Normal, that is, until they heard the sound of heavy feet pounding on the path outside, followed by Uncle Fred.

"Quick, back to the house," he said. He was breathing heavily, as he always did when he had to move his great bulk at speed. "We just got an e-mail. Videoconference with Himself in five minutes."

"But it's Friday!" said Joey—puzzled because videoconferences with the Big Cheese only happened on Tuesdays (rain or shine).

"I know," said Uncle Fred. "Something must have happened." He paused, gathering enough breath to carry on. "His e-mail had that phrase—the secret 'danger' phrase: 'Hotter than a cat's breath.' This could be serious."

The videoconference that Friday felt nothing like those that happened every Tuesday, rain or shine. For one thing, the humans weren't dressed for it. Normally they made an effort to look clean and pressed, with the men in shirts and ties, because that's the way the Big Cheese liked it.

But now, here they were, in their normal steamy clothes, with Uncle Fred's T-shirt decorated by a large ketchup stain from lunch, and the hint of a ketchup-colored tangle in his long beard.

On Tuesdays, the whole Mouse Council would be arrayed in a semicircle around their leader, but this time the Big Cheese was alone except for Sir Quentin, who was bowing to the webcam in his usual courtly fashion.

"If it's something secret, why is Sir Quentin there?" Megan whispered to Trey. "*You* could have interpreted."

"Must be trying to make the situation look normal," Trey whispered back. "In case there are eavesdroppers."

And indeed the meeting started off normally enough, with a speech of welcome.

"Sirs and madam," began Sir Quentin, "we are aware that you have accomplished yet another triumphant feat of engineering in the form of a second version of the Thumbtop, which could prove eminently useful in our combined efforts to combat climate change."

Megan glanced at the other humans and wondered if there was something she'd missed, because what possible connection could there be between Thumbtop Two and "hotter than a cat's breath"? The secret plea for help?

Uncle Fred seemed puzzled too.

"Hold on, sir. I'm not quite sure how—that is, I had really intended it for . . ."

The Big Cheese spoke again as Sir Quentin translated.

"Following our previous conversations on the subject," he said, while the humans looked at each other, baffled. Conversations? What conversations?

"Following those conversations, I have arranged that your visit to demonstrate the new device will take place this coming Monday at ten o'clock sharp. It will be a privilege to welcome at least two of you to our humble abode."

Jake started to say, "Now wait just a minute sir, we're not—"

Trey jumped onto his shoulder and gave him a sharp jab in the neck.

"Watch the boss," he whispered. "Look at him now."

As usual, when Sir Quentin reached the highest peaks of his rhetoric, he became so entranced by the river of sound flowing from his mouth that he closed his eyes. And as he launched into a speech about interspecies collaboration, the humans could see the Big Cheese saying again and again: "Please come." (It's both paws stretched out in front for the "please" part followed by the beckoning that means "come.")

Sir Quentin had stopped speaking, and the Big Cheese gazed straight into the webcam, waiting for an answer.

Uncle Fred tried another approach. "So, sir," he said, "can you give us an idea of the agenda for this meeting?"

"The agenda is not yet complete," said the Big Cheese, which was unusual because normally his agendas were ready to go well in advance.

Megan seized her chance. If the agenda wasn't fixed yet, then perhaps . . .

"So could we talk about my mom again?" she asked. "About telling her?"

The Big Cheese made a sign that could have meant either "Sure, sure" or "Don't bother me with that now"—the two front paws flapping without much conviction. Plainly, that wouldn't be the main focus of the meeting. So what would?

Sir Quentin closed his eyes as he translated the paw-flap into a speech beginning: "With regard to the possibility of enlightening the female parent," and the humans saw something that sent cold shivers down the backs of their necks, even in this heat.

As Trey whispered the translation behind Sir Quentin's back, the Big Cheese was saying something none had expected: "If you don't come, we may all die."

chapter four

When the videoconference was over that Friday, the four humans in Cleveland sat in silence for a minute, gazing at each other. Julia had jumped onto Megan's lap for comfort.

Was she trembling? Megan could understand how she must feel. Mice thought of the Big Cheese as all-powerful, and they liked it that way. Any crack in that armor would shake them deeply, and today he had seemed like one scared mouse.

Megan looked over at Trey, who shrugged.

"Don't ask me," he said. "No idea what's happening. No clue."

"Could you e-mail some friends?" asked Jake.

"No way," said Trey. "You know how fast rumors get around in human society? For mice, it's twice the speed. Wouldn't be good."

"But we have to find out what the problem is," said Uncle Fred.

"Hey, maybe there's an earthquake coming," said Joey. "California—that's big earthquake country. And animals get some warning, don't they?"

"If they do, it's probably only a couple of hours at most," said Jake. "Not days."

"Maybe the building's going to be torn down," Megan speculated, remembering her visit to Headquarters the year before. "It's sort of old."

"But why would that be such a secret?" wondered Jake.

"We have to go there to find out," said Uncle Fred, with a sigh. "We don't have a choice."

"I think we should both go, Fred," said Jake. "My guess is if it's just mice he's scared of, the Big Cheese could cope by himself. This must be bigger. Must involve humans in some way."

"Can't we all go?" asked Megan.

"Not really worth it," said Jake. "It'll be just a couple of days. You can both stay in my house and I'll get Cathy to move in and look after you. Okay? Then you guys can keep the factory going."

Cathy. The nice woman who cleaned his house. A babysitter.

"But, Dad," said Joey, "I might have a game on Monday."

"Ah yes," said Jake. "Monday. The little matter of baseball."

"No way you can miss that game, Jake," said Uncle Fred. "If Joey wins tomorrow, you *have* to go to the game on Monday. Then Megan could come with me. Right, Meg? You know your way around Headquarters!"

Well, yes, but that was when the Big Cheese was firmly in control. Not when his whole nation, his whole world seemed to be collapsing.

It was impossible to decide anything, of course, until Joey sorted out his "if/then" problem.

If his team won tomorrow, and *if* he and Jake went off to the next game on the road to the Little League World Series, *then* Megan and Uncle Fred would fly out to California.

And if the team lost tomorrow, then Megan and Joey would be stuck in Cleveland with a babysitter, while the two men went off on their adventure.

Some choice. Joey had to win.

They all went to Joey's game the next afternoon, which was a great way to stop worrying about Headquarters.

Curly and Larry never missed a game, of course. Jake had bought a hat with a tall crown, and he'd sewn two little hammocks into it so the mice could watch in comfort through the hat's eyelet holes.

Trey and Julia weren't normally crazy about baseball, but they couldn't miss *this* game, and watched it through little holes Megan had made in a pocket of her backpack.

Uncle Fred wasn't crazy about baseball either—college football was his passion. But that afternoon he got so involved that he kept leaping to his feet, to the great annoyance of the people behind him, because at his full height, Uncle Fred could blot out the sky.

For the first five innings the game was close, and Joey's team even fell behind by one run. Then, with two out in the last inning, Joey himself sent a double screaming past the third baseman to knock in two runs for the win.

Joey ended up under a pile of boys near home plate while everyone in Megan's section leaped to their feet and chanted "Jo-ey, Jo-ey," while Megan held her backpack high, and didn't care what people thought about it.

And the hat danced.

. . . .

"I'm *so* sorry I'll miss Headquarters," said Jake later that night as they celebrated at a Chinese restaurant, one that didn't mind if a cageful of mice had a chair to itself, with occasional pieces of noodle passing through the bars.

But Jake had a huge grin as he said it, so you could tell just how sorry he was that Joey's team would get to play at least one more game.

"I'm relying on you to look after your uncle, Megan," he said.

Megan guessed he was only half joking. Uncle Fred was a very smart guy, and if you put him in a garage with a bunch of tiny electronic parts, he could invent anything. And he was so big that when she was with him, she felt nothing terrible could happen to her. But he was not the most practical of humans, and if his mind was fixed on a new invention or something, he could seem terminally goofy.

"He's not safe out!" her mom had exploded once, when she'd asked her brother to return a book to the library and drop off some shirts at the dry cleaner's. He was thinking so hard about a new way to fasten a Thumbtop to a key ring that he'd pushed the clothes through the "return" slot at the library and hadn't realized his mistake until the dry cleaner told him she didn't clean books.

"Don't worry," Megan said now, reaching out to pat her uncle's hand. "We'll be fine."

Right.

There was one problem: what to do with the factory? Yes, the mice ran the assembly lines more or less by themselves, day and night, but there was always a panic button they could push if they had to send an alarm to a human cell phone.

True, no one had ever pushed the button, but if those phones were miles away when an emergency struck, who knew what could happen?

"We'd better stop the line for a couple of days," said Uncle Fred. "Give the workers a vacation."

"Do mice even take vacations?" wondered Jake as he reached out his chopsticks for the last piece of sweet-and-sour pork.

Joey had the dreamy look that meant his imagination was coming uncorked. "These guys can be the first. We could put some sand in a corner of the factory with those little umbrellas that people stick in drinks, maybe get a sunlamp and a big dish of water for them to wade in."

"You think?" said Jake, laughing.

"Listen to this," said Megan. She'd used the toothpick she

always carried to click on her Thumbtop, and brought up Whiskerpedia, the site where mice first look for answers to their questions. Peering through the magnifying glass that she wore around her neck, she read the entry under "Vacation."

Vacation

A period of enforced boredom and idleness. Humans pretend to enjoy "vacations," in which they roast their skin in the sun, travel to countries where the food upsets their digestion, immerse themselves in water until their pelt wrinkles, or inflict pain on their bodies with unaccustomed exercise.

"Fred, you want to tell them we're sentencing them to a vacation?" asked Jake.

"Let's give them a job instead," said Megan. "A different kind of job."

"Like what?" asked Joey.

Megan thought fast, and it came to her.

"Remember that idea my mom had, the week before she went to Green Stars?"

Jake nodded. "Sure. She was planning something for kids, like maybe a book on how climate change affects animals."

"Well, maybe the workers could do some of that research," said Megan. "And it could be sort of a gift for my mom, whenever the Big Cheese says we can tell her the truth."

"Works for me," said Jake. "'Welcome to our world, Susie, and here's everything you need for that book.'"

So it was decided. That evening, the four humans made a surprise visit to the factory to give the workers their urgent new task, one that would require them to use their brains rather than their paw-eye coordination.

The workforce would be divided into four teams, for mammals, birds, sea creatures, and insects. Each team would have access to four Thumbtops, and would use them to research the most endangered creatures they could find, digging up facts about their habitats, food and life cycles, and how these might be affected by climate change.

True, each individual mouse might have to wait a while for his or her turn at a Thumbtop. But at least it was just waiting. Not a dreaded vacation.

Early on Sunday morning, Jake and Joey dropped Uncle Fred and Megan at the airport. It took a while for all the good-byes because Curly and Larry were going off with Joey for his big game. Julia had always longed to see Headquarters, and would fly west with Megan even though that meant being separated from her clanmates for the longest time ever.

Trey looked on impatiently as the farewell huddle went on. And on. And on. Yes, yes, yes, those three were tied together by a powerful clan bond that meant they could never feel quite complete when they were apart for more than an hour or two. Trey envied them in a way, because the bond with his own clan had been broken early in life, when he'd been whisked away to the Talking Academy as a very young mouse. True, he'd found a clan of sorts there; he'd bonded with the other students. But that bond was nothing like this, which required five minutes of good-byes before Uncle Fred and Megan could check in for their flight.

And there were more delays at the check-in desk because there was no way—make that NO WAY—Megan could take those two mice on board; not in that cage, where all the passengers could see them and freak out because they looked like verm . . . They didn't even look like pets.

Uncle Fred had to buy the smallest animal carrier in the airport shop, one that was meant for cats. And Megan had to admit that it had its advantages. First, it was quite entertaining when people peered through the carrier's little mesh window with a, "Hey, kitty, kitty, kitty, EEEK!"

Second, this carrier was much more comfortable for mice than the old cage, which Uncle Fred stuffed into the overhead compartment.

And third, when the mice wanted to see out, Megan didn't have to unleash her braids so they could hide behind her hair, as she'd done on previous flights. Now she could just hold the carrier up to the window, and they all looked down together, checking for signs of climate damage.

Actually, America looked normal from here. The massive snows of last winter had melted, and the massive floods of spring had receded. While some forests had burned up in the heat last year, others still looked green, and in this part of the continent, at least, farmlands looked fertile.

"It's okay," Megan whispered. "I think you can save it."

Depending on what was really happening at Headquarters. Could it be something that threatened the very existence of the Mouse Nation? And with it, Operation Cool It? And with Operation Cool It, the planet?

chapter five

Megan had been dozing when something leaned over and squashed her against the plane's window: a large uncle who'd noticed that they were flying over mountains, and wanted a better look.

There was a map of America on his knees, and now he pointed to it and said, "I think your mom's right down there, or maybe a couple of valleys over."

You couldn't see much from up here, of course. They were too high over the Rockies to pick out anything that might be summer camps tucked into the woods. But what you could get from up here, Megan found, was guilt. How could she have forgotten, even in the excitement of packing and leaving, that today was Sunday? That her mom would have driven far out of her valley to a place where cell phones worked so she could make her only weekly call? To her only daughter?

Megan couldn't wait to get to San Francisco, hoping her mom would linger outside the valley today, waiting.

But she didn't.

Megan turned on her phone as the plane taxied to the gate, and all she could get out of it was a voice mail that (if she'd been a mouse) would have shriveled her whiskers or put a kink in her tail, big time.

"Hey, where are you?" said her mom. "I'm really mad at you for leaving your phone off! Didn't we agree that you'd keep it on every Sunday? It's just one day a week, kiddo—is that too much for you to remember? Can't hang around here all day—I'll send you an e-mail before I go back to camp."

Megan felt herself going red, because that's what happened when she felt guilty or mad, and now she felt both, though the mad part was at herself.

Uncle Fred gave her a hug. "Let's wait till we see what's in her e-mail," he said. "Then you can send her a voice mail. Even if she won't get it till next Sunday, it'll show you tried."

"But what can I tell her?" Megan asked. Not the truth, for sure.

"Tell her you'll explain next Sunday," he said. "Hey, maybe by then you *can* tell her the truth! Maybe you'll have permission."

Yes, that was a thought to hold on to.

. . . .

Deep in Silicon Valley, the Big Cheese had spent this weekend pretending that Headquarters was getting ready for a normal meeting, under normal circumstances, following the normal rules of mouse protocol. And as part of that preparation, he was choosing the official interpreter for the meeting.

Sir Quentin had been first to try out.

"I am familiar with the necessity for dignity," he began. "It is such an enduring honor to be engaged in this bi-species enterprise, this fruitful collaboration. . . ."

The Big Cheese let him rumble on for a couple of sentences, then thanked him and called for Savannah–Talking Mouse Seven. When she'd arrived at Headquarters a couple of months ago, he had been secretly amused by her antics. At least she was different, sashaying around on her hind feet with a pink bow pasted to her head! True, since he'd sent out that memo she'd been mostly back on all fours. And according to her performance evaluations, she was working harder at her job in the Training Department, helping young mice to understand human speech.

But now, at the prospect of meeting humans, she'd reverted to her old ways, walking on her hind legs with an extra swivel to the hips. As she stopped in front of her boss, she reached up with one paw to tweak the pink bow.

"Like, I talk modern?" she said. "Like a real human? From,

you know, totally this century? I'll be all, 'Hi, guys! My name is Savannah and I'll be your spokesmouse for today!'"

She looked at the Big Cheese sideways as if expecting applause—but all she got was a deep sigh of disapproval. Hadn't she learned to behave like a mouse after all? Did she have no sense of dignity? No sense of occasion?

"If there is one thing we need, small as we are," he said, "it is gravitas. Heft. We cannot let our guests of honor think we are a bunch of . . . of flibbertigibbets. Talking Mouse Five will be the interpreter on this occasion."

"Aw!" said Savannah, coming down onto all fours. "Anytime you want a flibberti . . . what you said, I'll be your mouse, okay?"

The Big Cheese sighed again as the two mice left, then went on to the next part of his preparations: hearing the ceremonial song from the Youth Chorus. The young mice shuffled in and, at a signal from the Master of Mouse Music, lurched into their signs. But they didn't have it quite right. Instead of:

Welcome, dear humans!

a couple of mice made the signs for:

Hi there, clunky mammals!

And when the words were meant to go:

> *Your factory for Thumbtops*
> *Is cooling the earth!*

someone signed:

> *Your factory for Thumbtops*
> *Is making planet ice cream!*

"They'll know their words tomorrow," said the Master of Music. "I guarantee it."

And he was surprised that the boss didn't seem too upset. In fact he'd hardly seemed to be watching, as if something much weightier than song was pressing on his brain.

Uncle Fred aimed the rented Prius southward on the freeway that led to Silicon Valley, and for the first twenty miles it was way too scary for Megan to even think about reading the e-mail from her mom.

As she knew all too well, freeways and Uncle Fred were not a good mix.

"I don't know what it is with Fred and cars," her mom had said. "He understands mechanical things, so you'd think he'd be a good driver."

You'd think wrong. Uncle Fred liked his mechanical things very, very small. He and cars did not get along. He only drove when he had to, and on this freeway he stayed in the slow lane, lurching from one side of it to the other, leaning forward and gripping the wheel in both hands while trucks roared past.

They were more than halfway to Silicon Valley before he made peace with the Prius, and Megan felt relaxed enough to click on the e-mail from her mom. She read it aloud:

Subject: Grrrrr

Hey, I've calmed down a bit since I left you that voice mail. But next Sunday . . .
     If you'd answered your phone we could have talked about the new campers who arrived yesterday. I told you Daisy Dakota was coming, didn't I?

Megan broke off her reading. "Remember her, Uncle Fred? In *Island Princess*? Daisy Dakota—she must be just about the most famous teenager on the planet!"

Megan went back to her reading:

Daisy is SO much smarter than people think,
which is great because every kid in America will
follow her lead. Oh yes, and Rocky Stone's here. I
guess Joey's a fan of his. Great action hero.
Tell Jake I wore it, and it was a big hit. Talk to
you next Sunday. Right? That's an order!

"Tell Jake she wore what?" asked Megan.

"I guess he gave her some blob jewelry," said Uncle Fred.
"Smart move. Hey, if the movie stars see those blobs, and want
some themselves, every woman in America will buy them too."

Of course. Blobs going Hollywood—that would be great for
business. But Megan was having trouble imagining her mom
wearing any jewelry, even Jake's solar earrings and bracelets and
necklaces that glowed deep into the night. Because, as far back
as she could remember, she'd never seen her mom with any
sort of jewelry. Ever.

They'd almost reached the turnoff for their hotel when Trey
yelled, "There it is!" and Julia ran up Uncle Fred's beard and
perched on his head to see where Trey was pointing.

And Uncle Fred almost lurched the Prius off the road.

"What the . . . ?" he said.

"It's Great America!" said Megan, craning her neck to see the towering Ferris wheel and the tops of some of the scariest roller-coaster rides in the world.

"And?" said Uncle Fred.

"And we have unfinished business here," said Trey. "Me and Megan. We only had time for that one ride—on the Demon. Remember, Megan?"

Remember? When that roller coaster had given her the worst ride in her life—in anyone's life—because Joey had just accidentally heard Trey talk? And she'd had no clue what he might do about it, but was terrified that he might lead some cops to Headquarters? *That* ride?

Oh yes. Great America owed her and Trey a ride or two that they could enjoy in peace, or even hate in peace, without the worries of that eventful day last year.

"Can we go there, Uncle Fred?" she asked now. "We have time."

"I guess," he said. "Just don't expect *me* to leave the ground. We've had a long and happy relationship, me and gravity, and I want to keep it that way."

. . . .

Right after they checked into their hotel, they set off for Great America.

Megan was wearing her mouse-transportation jacket, with tiny pieces of mesh sewn over holes in her pockets so mice could breathe and see out. The pockets were calm at first as Megan took them on a water ride, then a bumper car, then a sudden fall from the Drop Tower. But on the Demon, both pockets lost it, with wild wriggles and anguished squeaks from one side, and shouts of "Yikes!" from the other. Luckily, these sounds were covered up by the cacophony of human screams, including several from Megan herself. Because the ride was every bit as nasty as she remembered it.

While Megan and the mice were splashing and dropping and bumping, then spinning upside down above Uncle Fred's head, he took advantage of the crowds to do some market research. When Megan staggered off the Demon, her knees weak, she found him sitting on a bench with a crowd around him as he showed off Thumbtop Two.

"They all want one," he told her proudly. "I'm telling them to check out the Planet Mouse Web site so they can be the first on their block to have a phone on a key ring. And not just a phone, right?" he reminded his audience, raising a finger for attention. "A full computer to boot. Literally. Get it? To boot. That's a joke. You boot it up."

He gave his deep beard-shaking laugh, and the humans smiled indulgently because he fit their idea of a crazy inventor so perfectly.

"You have to go on at least one ride, Uncle Fred," said Megan when the crowd had drifted away. "It's the rules. Let's go on the Ferris wheel. It won't turn you upside down, I promise."

He agreed, reluctantly, and found that if he kept his eyes shut, he didn't even have to know how high up he was.

Until Julia climbed up his beard and held on to his hair with her back feet while she gently tried to pry one of his eyes open, because they had reached the top of the arc.

"Look, Uncle Fred!" said Megan. "Down there. You have to look."

He let Julia half open the eye, and indeed it was quite a sight in the dusk. To their west they could look down on the bright lights and noise and bustle of the park. But to their east lay the dark and silent building that housed the headquarters of the Mouse Nation.

"Saw it," said Uncle Fred, and closed the eye again. "It's headquarters."

Megan, Trey, and Julia gazed down at the empty building. Well, to humans it may have looked empty, but with their sharp eyes, the mice could make out the dim blue light that came from a few hundred Thumbtops, all at work.

"Wow," said Julia. (It's the right paw to the forehead.)

"Yes, wow," said Megan, who had learned that sign. "Bet they're all ready for us."

Well, yes and no . . .

Yes and no.

At Headquarters, everything that could have been done to prepare for the human visitors had been done. The agenda for the meeting was ready to be posted on the big computer in the conference room, the table had been polished to a deep shine by the scooting of a dozen mouse butts, the interpreter had been chosen, and the young mice who had messed up in the song were rehearsing overtime to get it right.

But nothing could allay the anxiety that was building up in the Big Cheese's mind; anxiety that went way beyond agendas and table polish and the words of songs. Something was deeply wrong, maybe too far gone for even humans to fix.

Could it be that after evolving as a society in which everyone worked for the common good—one for all and all for mice—the species Mus domesticus had evolved again? Making it possible for mice to turn on their own nation?

As he made his way to his bed—torn-up bits of newspaper on the bottom shelf of a bookcase—the Big Cheese remembered something that had been said by another ruler, hundreds of years ago.

He checked the quotation on his Thumbtop to make sure he had it right. Ah yes, here it was, from the Shakespeare play Henry IV, Part II:

Uneasy lies the head that wears a crown.

True, that line was written for a king, and not the leader of a rodent nation. And true, as a mouse, the Big Cheese didn't have a crown—just a piece of fine chain around his neck, which he took off at bedtime. But his head was certainly uneasy. Very uneasy indeed.

chapter six

After the long day of flying, followed by the long evening at Great America (not to mention the fact that it was way past her bedtime in Cleveland, where her body clock still thought it belonged), Megan just wanted to go to bed. But there was a holdup at the entrance to the hotel parking lot, because someone towing a trailer was having trouble turning around.

"Won't be long," said Uncle Fred, reading her mind.

A little green pickup truck with one fender painted a lighter green was stuck in the stream of traffic trying to leave the parking lot, its driver looking straight into their car. Megan glanced back at him in the way you do if you are waiting in traffic—just long enough to notice that he had a squashed-looking nose in a pinkish face, and not much hair. Megan would normally have looked away after that one glance, but something was happening to the face. Something big.

The man's small blue eyes went round as they lit up with recognition. He turned and said something to the woman beside him, and now both were staring.

Did she know them? But where from? In her sleepy state, Megan tried to think back over her recent life. Could they have been at one of Joey's baseball games in Cleveland? Or maybe at her dad's restaurant in Oregon last year? Or even on the Atlantic island where she'd lived while her mom was doing research on wild sheep?

The logjam of traffic sorted itself out, and Uncle Fred drove to a parking spot, but when Megan looked back toward the street, her *creep* alarm went off big time, because the green truck had done a quick U-turn and was coming back into the parking lot.

"Quick, Uncle Fred," said Megan, grabbing his spare hand as he locked the car, "there's a weird man."

"Hey, it's California," said Uncle Fred. "Lot of weird people here."

Then he saw that Megan was genuinely spooked, and hustled her into the hotel, then into the elevator. Just as the doors closed, they got a glimpse of a man with a pink face and a squashed-looking nose running into the lobby.

Uncle Fred pushed the buttons for every floor so that no one in the lobby could tell where they were getting off.

"Don't worry about it," he said. "Maybe he was just over-awed by your beauty."

She scowled at him because she this was no time for jokes. Even though people said she looked nice, nobody had ever accused her of being beautiful.

"Maybe he knows someone who looks like me?" she suggested.

"That must be it," said her uncle, grinning. "A dime a dozen, those Megans."

Meaning, of course, that you hardly ever saw eleven-year-old girls with braids, let alone red braids with bits of wiry hair always escaping. But then, not many girls Megan's age had mice to consider, with their need for handles when they're riding on a shoulder.

Uncle Fred saw that her *creep* alarm was still going strong.

"Hey, what makes you think you're so special?" he asked, giving her a hug. "He saw me too, didn't he? Probably recognized both of us, from that TV show?"

Yes, that must be it. Of course. The *Mouse Uses Computer* show that the Big Cheese had set up last year as part of the nice soft trap to catch Uncle Fred. No big deal.

. . . .

Megan put on her best clothes the next morning because Trey had told her that's what the Big Cheese expected at formal meetings.

True, last year she'd been wearing jeans. That day, the only way she could get to Headquarters was to tag along with Joey and his friends on their visit to Great America, slipping away through a secret gate in the fence. The boys would have thought her even weirder than they already did if she'd gone to Great America wearing anything like this—a dress with its own jacket, and shiny shoes.

"You guys going to a wedding?" asked the waitress at breakfast.

"Just a meeting," said Uncle Fred, who'd squeezed himself into his only suit.

"You don't see a lot of suits around here," said the waitress with a laugh. "Not in Silicon Valley. Not even for meetings."

Except for meetings with mice.

When they reached the cluster of office buildings behind Great America, Megan got out of the car to punch a combination of numbers into the gate that guarded Headquarters. They parked

near a side door and found the key that had been left beside it, under a piece of tile. Megan unlocked the door and pulled it wide.

"This is it?" asked Uncle Fred.

Megan had tried to prepare him. Headquarters was, after all, an old office building, and when you are only a few inches tall, there's no way you can paint walls, or clear out abandoned bits of junky furniture.

"What did you expect, the Magic Kingdom?" she whispered, because that's what Trey had whispered to *her* in this same spot last year.

They followed a guide mouse down the corridor to a strange sound—a fanfare of trumpets coming from synchronized Thumbtops stationed at intervals along the walls. True, the sound was pretty bad because the speakers on a Thumbtop are tiny, but the humans got the point. This visit had been officially declared to be a big deal.

The mouse led them to the conference room, which was familiar to Megan from last year, with its long table that was polished to a high gloss that reflected the waiting mice. At the far end was the Big Cheese himself, with the members of the Mouse Council arranged on either side, each with a red thread around his neck.

There was just one wrong note in this dignified scene: the mouse with a pink bow taped to her head. Savannah. As soon as Uncle Fred and Megan sat on the two chairs that had been put out for them, she sprinted across the tabletop.

"Oh, you big old humans, am I ever glad to see you!" she said in a breathy voice as she skidded to a stop in front of them. Megan smiled at her and was about to say "Hi" when Trey whispered a warning "Hush!" in her ear, while Julia, on her other shoulder, actually dug in her claws a little bit, because, as Megan knew, she would have killed to be the first female talking mouse ever.

"Silence!" roared the Big Cheese, translated by Sir Quentin. (You roar by stamping with your right back paw as you make your signs.) "Our greeting ceremony is not the time for individual manifestations. Talking Mouse Seven will return to her post *immediately*."

"I want to be your friend!" whispered Savannah. "Can you get me out of here?"

Then she scooted back to her place while Megan watched the Big Cheese, wondering what effect this disruption of the proceedings would have on him. None, apparently. He simply raised a paw and held it for a full twenty seconds as the quiet dignity that usually reigned at Headquarters reestablished itself.

"Now," he said finally, "let us begin."

He waved his paw, and the Youth Chorus lurched into its welcoming song, as Trey whispered the translation:

Welcome, dear humans
We greet you with mirth.
Your factory for Thumbtops
Is cooling the earth.
We can talk all we like
When we get Thumbtop Two.
It works both for paws
And for mouths, if you're you.

"Thank you, thank you," said Uncle Fred, and fished the prototype of Thumbtop Two out of his pocket. He was about to slide it across the table to the Big Cheese, when Trey hissed, "Not till Item Four."

That prompted Megan to check the agenda that was posted on the big computer in the corner:

1. Welcoming Song
2. Opening Remarks
3. Possible Enlightenment of Fifth Human
4. Demonstration of Thumbtop Two

5. Progress of Operation Cool It

6. Other Business

The opening remarks, as translated by Sir Quentin, droned on. And on. And on. "Your long journey . . . our humble abode . . . interspecies collaboration . . ."

Megan wasn't really listening, because who could? She glanced at Uncle Fred and wondered if he was having the same thought as she was. Where on that agenda was the real reason for their journey to Silicon Valley? The threat to the whole nation? Something hotter than a cat's breath?

All she got from her uncle was the slightest of shrugs. No clue.

And soon that thought was driven out of Megan's head by a more urgent one. Item Three was coming up fast, and she'd have to speak, making the case for telling her mom the truth. And not just to the Big Cheese this time, but to his whole silent council, which she found quite intimidating. Megan had rehearsed the argument over and over in her head. How valuable her mom would be to the nation and to Operation Cool It because of her great knowledge about climate change. How hard it was for the human young to keep important secrets from their parents. But she'd tried these arguments before. Would they be enough today?

". . . business success . . . recent innovation . . ." Sir Quentin droned on.

And if she *did* get permission to tell her mom, how should she actually do it? Like on the phone, next Sunday? Or what if Joey's team lost and Jake was free to drive them to Oregon by way of Camp Green Stars, could she do it then? Take her mom for a walk in the woods, with Trey, far enough from camp so the movie stars wouldn't hear any EEEEKs. . . .

". . . technical infrastructure . . . climate modification . . ."

Of course she'd have to make sure her mom was sitting down before she said, "Mom, Trey has something to tell you." And she could finally stop lying to her mom, stop dodging the truth.

"In conclusion," Sir Quentin was saying.

Even from him, those words usually meant an end was in sight, and it would be her turn. Would she go red? That sometimes happened when she had to read a report in class. It was bad enough to blush in front of fifth graders—but just try it with mice. When a mammal changes color—not just some dumb chameleon or something, but a real *mammal*—mice are so astonished by the sight that they forget to be polite. And all these mice would stare. Maybe there'd even be some "Laughing out loud" or "Holy cow" signs from the Youth Chorus, which would make her go redder than ever.

Sir Quentin had indeed concluded.

In the silence, Megan could feel her heart beating as she waited for the Big Cheese to give a signal. And yes, now he tapped the side of his head with the left paw three times. The third item on the agenda. Her turn.

"You're on!" whispered Uncle Fred. "Go for it!"

"It's like this," she began, hearing her voice far too loud in this silent place, feeling the beginning of warmth in her cheeks, which could mean that the worst was happening. "Sir, I know that you think my mother . . ."

Her voice trailed off. The assembled mice were not gazing in awe at her reddening face after all. Instead, they had swiveled their heads in the direction of the door, where a messenger mouse had appeared—a mouse with a Thumbtop strapped to his back. Megan watched as the mouse took a leap up onto a chair, and from there to the table.

"Keep going," said the Big Cheese (it's a sort of winding motion of the tip of the tail), but he didn't seem at all interested in anything she had to say. Instead, he was concentrating on the mouse who had now reached him and was turning around so his leader could read the message on his Thumbtop.

Uncle Fred whispered, "What the . . . ?" as he leaned forward, waiting.

The Big Cheese finished reading, then gazed straight at the humans as if they could, and should, read his thoughts. But what he said seemed like a total anticlimax.

"Forgive me, Miss Megan, if we briefly postpone the discussion of your parent. I have rearranged the agenda, so we will turn now to Item Four. Mr. Barnes, please show us the new Thumbtop."

"Okay," said Uncle Fred, sliding the Thumbtop across the table, making the "Okay" long and drawn out and rising up at the end, sort of "O . . . kaaay?" Meaning, *This may all sound normal on the surface, sir, but we both understand something very weird is going on.*

But when the new computer arrived in front of the Big Cheese, he patted it with his paws as if nothing strange were happening.

"This is the model with telephone capability, sir," said Uncle Fred. "Allow me to describe its new features."

"Why describe when we can demonstrate?" asked the Big Cheese. "Talking Mouse Three, come with me. And Mr. Fred, please turn on your cell phone so you can be sure to hear when we call you."

Megan held Trey up near her ear.

"Don't worry," he whispered. "This time it's cool."

Not like on that first visit, when he'd been whisked away from this conference room to go work in the Training Department and she thought she'd lost him forever.

Trey climbed down to the tabletop and ran to stand in front of the Big Cheese, where a couple of muscle mice fitted him with a harness and lifted the Thumbtop Two into it. Then he and the Big Cheese headed for the edge of the table, hopped down to a chair, then to the floor, and were gone.

chapter seven

There are silences and then there are Silences. This was one of the second variety, a Silence in which the humans could almost hear their hearts beating. From the outside world came the happy screams of Great America, but in the foreground—nothing—nothing to distract Megan from her thoughts, which were tumbling around in an uncomfortable tangle. Was the Big Cheese just *bored* with the subject of her mom? Would she really get Trey back? What *was* going on?

She looked at the members of the Mouse Council. No clues there. They were sitting just as still as she was, not even looking at each other. She turned to Uncle Fred, who shrugged and nodded toward the silent cell phone on the table. Be patient. Wait.

Big help.

The silence seemed to last forever but in fact it was only a minute or two before Uncle Fred's phone rang. It was set on

SPEAKER so everyone heard the message—Trey's voice loud and clear, saying, "Mr. Watson, come here. I want to see you."

Which brought a deep chortle from Uncle Fred.

"That's so smart," he said. "That's what Alexander Graham Bell said in the first-ever phone call, human to human. And this is the first-ever call from a mouse to a human. Works for me."

Then he stopped smiling at the phone's next words, which were, "A word in your ear, please."

Uncle Fred turned off the speaker and held the phone to his ear, swiveling to look at Megan as he did so. Then he stood up and gestured for her to stand up too.

"We'll be there," he said.

Megan felt huge again as she followed Uncle Fred out of the conference room, with Julia clinging to a braid.

"Second corridor to the right," whispered Uncle Fred. "That's what Trey said. And we're to make sure we're not followed. Can you believe it?"

As if he were taking part in a game, he tiptoed with exaggerated care down the corridor ahead of Megan, spinning around every few steps to make sure there was no one—no mouse—behind them. And indeed no one followed as they turned into the second corridor on the right. There was no sign of life in this corridor either, until they saw a solitary mouse standing outside a door that was different from the rest—the door to a broom closet. Trey.

"Julia," he said, as they came close. "You keep guard. Tell us if anyone gets near enough to overhear."

He waved the humans through the door and into the broom closet, which Uncle Fred seemed to fill from top to bottom. Megan noticed he was wearing the same expression that he'd had last year, when he first learned that mice had evolved. A little worried, yes, but mostly overjoyed to be right in the middle of the greatest science fiction movie of all time.

The Big Cheese was standing beside Thumbtop Two—and it was lucky that he was still wearing his fine chain of office around his neck, because without it, Megan would never have recognized him.

This was not the leader of a proud nation.

This was one scared mouse, who seemed to have lost all his gravitas.

"It's bad stuff," said Trey, as the humans squatted down to be nearer to mouse level. "Look."

"When I summoned you last Friday," said the Big Cheese. "It was because I had just received this message from one of our operatives in the county offices. The office that deals with pests."

He clicked on the Thumbtop and brought up an e-mail:

From: SC87409@mousenet.org
To: Topmouse@mousenet.org
Subject: Report of infestation

Sir, I thought you ought to know about an e-mail
that just came in. It says: "Did you know there's a
building behind the Great America theme park that
has a massive mouse infestation? There are thirty-
two mice in one office and thirty-six in the next. I
think this is disgusting and you should send in the
exterminators."

"This building?" exclaimed Uncle Fred. "But who could
have reported you? Like a delivery person or something? Some
mailman looking through a window?"

"It was not a mailman," said the Big Cheese. "All our offices
open onto an interior court, so none have windows humans
can look through."

Megan was ahead of him, and a cold feeling seemed to wrap
itself around her insides. If it wasn't a human. . . .

"It was a mouse!" she said. "You think it was a mouse!"

"I *know* it was a mouse," said the Big Cheese sadly. "Because
that e-mail gave the authorities information no human could

have known—the precise mouse-count in two adjoining offices. In due course, I am confident that we can identify the wrong-doers, though now is not the time."

Uncle Fred stood up, hitting his head on the low ceiling, then crouched down again.

"Well, we're here to help," he said. "What would you like us to do? Go to the county offices and ask them to please stop looking for you?"

That brought a quick "Laughing out loud" sign, though it was made abruptly, without humor.

"That might have been a good plan," said the Big Cheese, "but it is now too late. It is too late because of *this*."

He brought up another e-mail—the one the messenger mouse had brought into the conference room:

From: SC87409@mousenet.org
To: Topmouse@mousenet.org
Subject: DANGER

The pest control people have guessed which building is 'infested,' and exterminators are coming to HQ this p.m.

"We must evacuate the premises immediately," said the Big Cheese. "And it is fortunate, is it not, that on the day the exterminators come, we have humans to help us—humans with wheels?"

"Whoa!" said Uncle Fred. "You mean our Prius? Maximum capacity five humans or maybe eight hundred mice? How many are you?"

"The latest census put our population at two thousand two hundred and forty-three," said the Big Cheese.

"We can rent a bigger car, right?" said Megan. "We *have* to save them, Uncle Fred!"

"I don't think any regular car would be big enough," said Uncle Fred. "Not even an SUV. We'll have to rent an RV. A recreational vehicle. A dirty great house on wheels. How long do we have?"

"Leave now," said the Big Cheese, drawing himself up to his tallest as if to make the point that even though he needed help from humans, he was still, after all, the leader. "I will give the order to prepare for evacuation."

He leaned forward and tapped out a brief e-mail on the Thumbtop. Before he pushed SEND, he invited the humans to read it. It didn't take long.

From: Topmouse@mousenet.org
To: Allmicehq@mousenet.org
Subject: Evacuation Drill

All mice will follow evacuation drill, to be completed no later than twelve noon.

When he'd read it, Uncle Fred reached out his hand to touch what should have been the most powerful paw on the planet, except that now it was trembling as the Big Cheese gazed imploringly at the humans who were his only hope.

By the time Megan and Uncle Fred had scooped up their two mice and reached Main Street, the evacuation message had reached the emergency response team, and the alarm was sounding, sharp and loud, the same old bicycle horn that had warned Headquarters last year that Megan was on the loose, hunting for Trey.

Then, it had sounded only once. Now there were three blasts on the horn, each louder than the last:

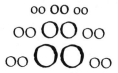

Megan realized she'd never be able to give Uncle Fred a proper tour of Headquarters. Never show him the amazing research that went on there, because now the core of mouse civilization would be dismantled, packed up for evacuation. Already, as they hurried past open offices on Main Street, they could see mice pulling charts off walls where they'd been pinned, low down. Thumbtops were being lined up in the doorways of each office, ready to go. And mice were scurrying every which way as if—well, as if their lives depended on it.

It's amazing how fast you can move when you have to. And one of the things about moving fast to stay ahead of a looming emergency is that you don't bother to check whether anyone is following you. You don't notice whether or not a green pickup truck is sliding away from its parking spot as your Prius goes by.

Uncle Fred and Megan hurried back to the hotel to pack and check out while Trey and Julia hid under the seat of the Prius with a Thumbtop, booking an RV. As Trey often said, on the Internet, nobody knows you're a mouse, and by the time Megan and Uncle Fred ran out of the hotel, trundling their suitcases, Trey had used Uncle Fred's credit card to reserve a vehicle that could accommodate at least 2,423 mice—2,425 if you included Trey and Julia.

After that it was easy.

They turned in the Prius at its rental company and took a taxi to the RV place, where Trey had booked a shiny silver RV that blew Megan's mind—so huge, so tall, and so enticing, with all its closets and bathroom and kitchen, and seats that turned into beds. But Uncle Fred looked decidedly daunted as he piloted the thing off the lot and into the traffic in a series of jerks and lurches that made Julia and Trey cower down in the cup holders where they were traveling.

They jerked their way into the parking lot of a strip mall, where Uncle Fred used up at least three parking spaces as they bought two big bags of mouse food plus kitty litter and two trays to spread it on. Then Uncle Fred hurried into an office

supply store to buy a couple of cardboard boxes, each big enough to transport one mouse research team at a time.

The parking lot by Headquarters was still blessedly empty, and Headquarters itself was calm. Megan had half expected to find scenes of panic, or at least frantic activity, but if there had been any, it was over. Main Street was paved with phalanxes of mice waiting politely for deliverance, each with a sign-mouse in front carrying a piece of card glued to a wooden matchstick with the name of a department: Accounting, Business, Climate, Cool It, Crop Futures, Education, Engineering, Forward Planning—a score of departments in alphabetical order, plus the mousekeeping and security teams that kept Headquarters going.

Way down at the far end of Main Street, where the light was dim, Megan saw a glint of gold from a piece of fine chain as the Big Cheese, like the captain of a sinking ship, prepared to be the last to leave.

Loading everyone into the RV went fast. The humans would place a cardboard box on its side, a department would march in, stand absolutely still for the ride, then march out to stand in neat rows on the floor of the RV, waiting.

"Shouldn't we spread them out?" Megan asked, as the floor started filling up. "Maybe put some guys on the seats? Or the table?"

"Later," said Uncle Fred, almost sprinting back for another load. "Let's get them all out of here first."

It didn't take long to finish airlifting everyone to safety in the RV. *Almost* everyone. Megan was just emerging with the World Hunger Department, and Uncle Fred was way back at the other end of Main Street, collecting the Mouse Council and the Big Cheese himself when Trey saw it.

"Uh-oh," he whispered from Megan's shoulder.

Through the open doorway, he had seen a man pulling on a white jumpsuit of the sort people wear when they are working with very strong chemicals. And a van was parked next to the RV.

A white van with big letters on its side:

EXTERMINATOR
We'll Get the Best of Your Pest

chapter eight

he man in the white jumpsuit hadn't seen Megan yet, but was walking slowly toward the RV. In a couple of seconds he'd look through a window and see more mice than you could exterminate in a lifetime, all lined up in rows, the way they had been unloaded.

Megan's first instinct was to drop the box carrying the World Hunger Department and rush back to the protection of Uncle Fred, who was still way down at the other end of Main Street, scooping up the last box of mice. But that would be disastrous, of course—and Trey knew it.

"Say something!" he whispered urgently from her shoulder. "Distract him!"

"Hi there!" Megan called out. The man stopped advancing on the RV. But what came next? How could she possibly explain the box she was carrying? If it had a lid she could pretend it was office supplies, but lids don't work for rapid mouse transport, and she'd folded the top flaps down into the box to make it easier for the mice to march in. Now she started to rotate the box so the open side would be against her body, but she was too late. The man in the white suit took a couple of quick steps toward her.

"Hand over those mice, little lady!" he called out. "Don't try to kill them yourself! Leave that to the professionals!"

"No, it's okay," she said. "They're . . ."

What could she possibly say? That these mice were her friends? That they had evolved and were every bit as smart as he was?

It was Trey who gave her the words she needed. "Tell him we're an act!" he whispered. "Performing mice!"

"They're part of my act," Megan said.

"We perform at Great America," Trey whispered.

"We do a show at Great America," said Megan obediently.

And for the first time today she was glad to be wearing the new dress and the shiny shoes that made it look as if she were absolutely ready to go onstage, or wherever you go with a mouse act.

Another man was leaning against the van, pulling a white jumpsuit over his clothes.

"Take a look at this, Luis!" the first man called out. "She says those mice are part of an act. You ever hear of such a thing? Performing mice?"

The man called Luis came over, the top of his white suit still unzipped and hanging around his waist.

"No way!" he said. "Mice don't perform. Mice are dumb. Real dumb. Know what I always say about mice, Al?"

"The only good mouse is a dead mouse?" said Al.

"Yeah, that's what I always say," said Luis.

While they were talking, Trey whispered a new word into Megan's ear. *Robots.*

"They're robots," said Megan. "Robot mice. And this robot," she added, jerking her head toward Trey, "is programmed to give them instructions. Here, I'll show you."

She put the box on the ground then picked Trey off her shoulder and held him out on the palm of her hand, so the mice in the box could see his signs as he went into a series of stiff MSL commands. And on those commands, the World Hunger Department marched out of its box and divided into two sections, then four, like a human high school band, ending with slow pirouettes and deep bows in unison before marching back into the box.

"See?" said Megan, feeling braver. "No way real mice could do that."

"No way," agreed Luis.

"So that's what's in the building?" said Al. "Robots? Someone reported it was infested, but you're telling me it's just robots?"

"You got it!" said Megan.

"Well, isn't that the darnedest thing," said Luis. He'd zipped up his white suit but now he unzipped it again. "Never seen robots like that. Hey, I'll tell my kid. He's crazy for that sort of stuff. You'll be in that big theater place, right? What time are you on?"

That flummoxed Megan for a moment, because she had no

idea when shows happened at Great America, and she felt herself starting to go red. But at that moment Uncle Fred emerged from the Headquarters building, where he'd been listening in the shadows with the Big Cheese on his shoulder and the box holding the Mouse Council in his hands.

"Pretty good act, right?" he said to the men. "You can check the times on the Great America Web site."

He unloaded the Mouse Council onto the last empty piece of floor in the RV, lifting the Big Cheese into the little old birdcage, which he'd hung from the rearview mirror, its door tied open so no one could think the leader of the Mouse Nation was a prisoner.

"He's the chief robot," Uncle Fred explained to the exterminators. "Gets pride of place."

The two men had followed Uncle Fred to the RV, and although he was carefully blocking the doorway, they could plainly get a glimpse through the windows of the mouse-mass now covering the floor.

And if one mouse lost it . . .

Megan remembered Curly's account of being captured by Joey last year, before Joey learned the truth about mice. Curly had gone straight into WWAWMD mode: "What Would A Wild Mouse Do?" Because there is no way you should show any human (except for the four who Knew) how smart you are. If anyone decided on a strategy of WWAWMD right now, it could mean DEATH. But to Megan's relief, the rows of mice stood stock still, like robots on a toy-store shelf.

"I'd show you some of their moves," said Uncle Fred, "but we don't want to run the batteries down before the show."

Al had a goofy smile on his face, and Luis was shaking his head in admiration. "Well, good luck with it," he said. "We'll have to check out the building, of course, but hey, no rush."

"Megan, want to take a last look?" asked Uncle Fred. "Make sure there's no robot left behind?"

He handed Megan an empty box and sat firmly on the step of the RV so that no one could get any closer to his robots, while Megan checked Headquarters for anything that might give Luis and Al a hint that intelligent beings had lived there. There wasn't much—just a few sheets of paper taped to the walls at mouse height. A map of the Middle East. A financial report on cheese from The Economist. And a battered picture of a cat from the shooting range, where young mice with elastic bands had practiced catapulting paper clips at the enemy.

But there was one last thing Megan found that she couldn't clear out—the deepest mouse secret. A mountain of mouse poop piled high in a closet.

"Well, that's a dead giveaway," whispered Uncle Fred, when she told him. "We'd better get out of here before someone realizes robots don't poop. Did you know that? That robots don't poop?"

And he laughed hysterically in a way that made Megan wonder if the strain had been too much, finally.

When Megan looked back on that first hour after they pulled away from Headquarters and its exterminators, it was hard to decide which memory was worst.

Maybe if Uncle Fred had taken the time to get used to the huge RV. Maybe if they'd found a big empty parking lot where he could practice before diving into freeway traffic. Maybe if they'd had time for another meeting with the Big Cheese and sorted out a few things, like who was in charge now, and who was to make decisions, and where they were going, and how could the mice help, and who'd be responsible for keeping a lookout. Things like that.

Yeah, right.

It all could have happened, but for the poop. Within minutes, Luis and Al would find it and get word to the cops. We were lied to about those robots. Stop those robots. Those robots could be a health hazard. Those robots *poop*.

"Is it a crime?" Megan asked her uncle as he pitched the RV into the roaring traffic on the freeway. Did he actually shut his eyes for a moment as he merged in front of a massive truck that blared its horn in anger?

"What, a crime to carry a few thousand mice without seat belts? Or not reporting poop?" He laughed again with a new touch of hysteria. "Let's not stick around to find out."

He gunned the RV up to the same speed as everyone else on the freeway, which was much faster than his comfort zone.

If Uncle Fred was scary driving a Prius, the twenty-five-foot RV was even more exciting. First, there was the little problem of the gears. He'd always driven an automatic, so changing gears seemed to take forever, with metallic screams as the stubby little gear shift hunted for the right slot. Add to that the pedal problem: Uncle Fred wasn't used to three pedals, so whenever he had to change gears he'd look down at his feet while the RV lurched toward someone else's lane.

Megan tried one question: "Where are we going?"

"Thataway, I guess," said Uncle Fred. "East." He took a large hand off the wheel for just long enough to point dead ahead, as they jerked and swayed and wobbled and zigzagged their way along the bottom end of San Francisco Bay toward some golden-brown hills.

"To Cleveland?" she asked.

That brought a short laugh.

"Yeah, we might hit Cleveland," he said, "if it gets in our way."

Megan looked up at the Big Cheese swinging gently in his cage as he gazed straight ahead. Was he in shock? Or mesmerized by being out in the world for the first time in years? Or scared literally witless by Uncle Fred's driving? Hard to guess. His back seemed to be telling everyone that whatever was happening in the RV had nothing to do with him. Two thousand two hundred and forty-three highly intelligent mice heading who knew where? Not his problem.

A benevolent despot, that's what Jake had called the Big Cheese, which was like a dictator, but one who does good. If he was still that despot, Megan thought, still that dictator, could he please start to dictate? Take charge and somehow make everything come out right, the way he always seemed to do before?

"Sir?" she tried.

No answer.

She took a quick glance back into the depth of the RV, hoping that maybe some enterprising director might step into the vacuum—organize the brain-power and Thumbtop-power of his department, and come up with some sort of plan. But like their leader, the mice seemed to have been stuck in robot configuration, still standing in neat rows, looking straight ahead, as if they now expected the humans to make all the decisions.

And Uncle Fred was giving all his attention to the task of surviving the traffic.

"I'm calling Jake," Megan announced. Now, *there* was a human she could use—he'd know exactly what they should do next. But all she got was voice mail. Of course: Joey's game would be starting about now. She visualized Jake in his hat, watching Joey as he maybe pitched a shutout that would take his team toward the State Championship, toward the World Series, and she felt a stab of jealousy, because if only the Big Cheese hadn't made that cry for help, they might all be there at the game. Instead of here.

"I'm leaving a message for Jake," she said. But what message? She thought of saying, "Get out here *now*," or at least "We're on a freeway with two thousand mice. Help!" but she settled on something that wouldn't freak anybody out. "Hi there. Call us after the game. And hey, good luck to Joey."

chapter Nine

Megan reached up to touch the comforting form of Trey on her shoulder.

"We need a grown-up," she whispered.

The RV had made it to the east side of San Francisco Bay, and forced its way onto a freeway that was twice as busy as the one they'd left. And now Megan noticed something even more scary. Uncle Fred was starting to enjoy himself. She could even hear a soft "vroom-vroom" coming from under his beard as he pulled out to overtake a truck, flooring the accelerator to see just how fast the massive RV could go before lurching back into the slow lane.

And the Big Cheese? There was no movement in the cage. He stood still as a rock, gazing straight ahead.

"I've got news," whispered Trey as Uncle Fred vroom-vroomed to within inches of the truck in front before pulling out to pass it just a few feet ahead of a very angry SUV.

"I've got news," Trey repeated. "*You're* the grown-up."

"Oh, please," Megan said. "You're more of a grown-up than I am."

"Me?" said Trey. "Being fully grown doesn't always help—like when you need thumbs for finding a map? So we can get off this road?"

Megan used her thumbs to open the glove compartment and yes, there was a map of the Bay Area, and after she'd found their position on it, she saw a solution to their immediate problem. A way to get out of this traffic. A way to give them a sporting chance of staying alive.

"If we take the next exit, Uncle Fred," she said, "it'll get us onto a smaller road."

"So?" said Uncle Fred.

"It's a shortcut," she said, "toward Cleveland. We'll need to get off this road in about a mile."

"Sounds good," he said. "If I can get into the exit lane."

Megan checked the right-hand mirror for him and saw two things: First, it was safe for the RV to move into the exit lane. Second, a familiar-looking vehicle was right behind them.

A little green pickup truck.

"Trey," Megan whispered, a prickling feeling starting in her feet and running up to her head. She pointed at the mirror. "Can you see . . . ?"

"Uh-oh," he said, peering at the mirror. "I'm on it."

He ran off toward the back of the RV, taking the high route over countertops and seats to stay above the ranks of mice on the floor. Megan turned to watch him pull aside a piece of the blind that blocked the back window. He looked out, then sprinted back to her.

"It's definitely him," he said. "The guy from the hotel. Pink face. Squishy nose. Woman in the passenger seat. Small green truck with light green fender. But it could be a coincidence, right? They could just *happen* to be on this road?"

Well, maybe. But when Uncle Fred steered the RV into the exit lane, was it a coincidence that the green truck moved into that lane too? And when Uncle Fred turned off the freeway onto the smaller road, and the little green truck turned right behind him—coincidence?

Megan put her head down in her hands with an "Aaargh" sound.

"What's up?" asked Uncle Fred. "Don't like my driving, suddenly? Or is this the wrong road?"

"It's that man," she said. "From last night. He's following us!"

"The guy in the . . . can't be. Can it?"

He jammed his foot down on the accelerator, but that brought another problem. This new road followed the bends of a small river, and it only took one big bend at speed for mice to start flying. And soon the floor of the RV had become a wriggling, wrestling morass of mice, flopping into furry piles so you couldn't see which tail belonged to which set of ears.

And even going as fast as he dared, there was no way Uncle Fred could outrun the green truck.

"Trey!" wailed Megan. "Think of something!"

"We have three options, as I see it," he said. "One, let him catch up with us at some point, then maybe organize some sort of mouse attack to make sure his truck breaks down."

And let him see the cargo? Report it to the police?

"Two—we can ask the Big Cheese to call a meeting right now," Trey whispered. "Maybe discuss the situation with the Mouse Council and draw up a plan."

Megan looked up at the Big Cheese, still gazing ahead like a stuffed mouse. Hard to imagine any plans coming out of him in the near future.

"Or?"

"Or lose him right now. Get away from him. Let's look at that map."

Megan studied it. Yes, there was the bridge they'd just crossed. So a couple of miles farther on, where the map showed a side road . . .

She pointed to the road. "You think?"

"Let's check it out on Google Maps," said Trey. "Where's your Thumbtop?"

Megan held it out for him, and he quickly found the right part of California and zoomed in on the satellite view of the road.

"Perfect," he said. "Look, it's not far to that grove of trees, then there's a place to turn off."

"Let's do it," she said.

Trey hopped over to Uncle Fred's shoulder.

"We'll be leaving this road soon," he said. "But first, slow down on the next straight bit. The green guy probably won't overtake you, but maybe someone will overtake *him*."

And that's what happened. The stream of traffic behind the RV readjusted itself on the straight bit of road, with cars hustling to get in front of each other so they could overtake the RV. Except for the green truck. It held back, letting a couple of cars pass.

As they approached the next bend, Trey directed Uncle Fred to speed up—to take the bend as fast as he could, then spin off onto the side road that would open up to their right.

"Vroom-vroom!" came from the beard as Uncle Fred gunned the massive vehicle forward, then spun the wheel so suddenly that Megan was afraid they might tip over. The Big Cheese rocked hard in his cage and wrapped his paws tight around the bars to keep from falling out. Mice piled up like snowdrifts in the corners of the RV, while Trey grabbed a piece of beard and Julia swung wide on a braid.

The side road was just as good as it had looked on Google Maps. It kept dividing and dividing so that even if the green truck had managed to do a U-turn and follow them, old Squishy-nose wouldn't know which way to turn.

Still going as fast as he dared, Uncle Fred took an unpaved farm road and tucked the RV behind a clump of eucalyptus trees. And then, blessedly, he stopped.

After he'd turned off the engine, he sat for a while as the silence settled around them, except for the slight squeaking of the old birdcage still rocking as it dangled from the mirror.

He unbuckled his seat belt and put his head down on the steering wheel, his shoulders shaking. Megan laid a tentative hand on his back. Had it all become too much? Was Uncle Fred actually *crying*? An uncle his size? But then sounds began to emerge from the beard, first a sort of whimpering that could have gone along with crying, but then the unmistakable sounds of laughter.

Whether it was the shock of all that lurching, or the relief that it had stopped, something seemed to flip a switch in the Big Cheese and bring him back to life. He turned to the solid mass of mouse that was carpeting the floor of the RV, and gave an order that Trey relayed into Megan's ear.

"He's saying, 'Everyone—express your interspecies solidarity with Mr. Fred by laughing out loud, even if you have to fake it.'"

Which the mice did. It's easy for mice to fake laughter, of course, because it's just the paw to the mouth with three quick taps on the lips, but as Megan watched 2,243 mice (or at least those who were not upside down) go through the motions in unison, she noticed that gradually real laughter swept through the RV. More and more mice lost it, rolling over on their backs with their paws tapping away at their mouths in a paroxysm of mouse giggles.

"Know what?" Megan began.

At Trey's suggestion, the two humans had left the RV to allow the second most powerful species on earth to sort itself out and retrieve some of its lost dignity. Now the humans were sitting on the dry and crunchy grass of late summer, leaning against a comforting rock in the shade of the eucalyptus grove.

"I think we just killed two cats with one stone," she said.

Uncle Fred laughed. "Cat one, getting away from that guy, right?" he said. "What's the second cat?"

"Giving the mice time to sort themselves out."

"Don't forget cat three!" said Trey, from Megan's knee.

"Huh?" said Megan.

"Getting the Big Cheese to take charge," he said.

And, yes, that was an important cat. Before they'd even left the RV, the Big Cheese had climbed onto the back of the driver's seat and started ordering his followers to untangle themselves and form up again in their departments. Mouse discipline was restored. Definitely a good cat.

It was Julia who saw the signal from a lookout mouse, and gave Trey a quick pat to draw his attention to it.

"We're being summoned," he said. "Back to the Mousemobile."

"Mousemobile," said Uncle Fred. "I like that. Do they need help?"

Certainly not. Mice never ask for help unless they absolutely have to. When the humans climbed back into the Mousemobile, they found that the organization of mice was complete. Each department had been assigned a place to ride on a bed or a bench or a countertop, so it was now possible to walk from one end of the Mousemobile to the other without squashing anyone.

And getting the Big Cheese to take command? That had happened too, as the humans found when he summoned them for a private talk. At a sign from the Big Cheese, Uncle Fred held the cage down low so none of the other mice could see their leader doing something unheard of: apologizing.

"Forgive me," he began, as Trey whispered the translation. "When we took to the road, I thought it best to abdicate my responsibility because we are, after all, on your territory, and in your power. I therefore thought it best to leave all leadership in your hands."

"Well, we're happy to have you take charge again, sir," said Uncle Fred. "And we would welcome your lead in plotting a route."

"Thank you," said the Big Cheese. "We have indeed drawn up plans for the immediate future. My Director of Geography has plotted a way to reach the city of Tracy unobserved, on side roads that cut through these hills. On the outskirts of that city, using the Nation's credit card—which is, as you will recall, in *your* name—we have booked connecting rooms in a motel. We chose it because Google Maps shows that even a vehicle of this size can park at the back, out of sight. Once we are unloaded, and there is no trace of our presence anywhere in this vehicle, you will exchange it for another. My Director of Transportation has already been in touch with the local rental agency, which is expecting you."

Uncle Fred's beard went south as his jaw dropped.

"Why look so surprised?" asked the Big Cheese. "You will agree that this plan will get us out of our current predicament, and ensure that your pursuer, whoever he is, will lose the trail. And we are, after all . . ."

Uncle Fred finished the thought before Trey could get to the end of his translation.

"You are, after all, mice," he said with a huge grin. "Let's roll!"

And Megan could almost feel his relief that mice were taking charge.

chapter ten

I t took all of Uncle Fred's skill to pilot the Mousemobile along the narrow farm roads that led them between the golden hills of high summer to safety, guided by a geography mouse with Google Maps on his Thumbtop.

At last they emerged from the hills onto a better road, and from there it was not hard to find the motel where Mr. Barnes had reserved two adjoining rooms, well out of sight at the back. And while Megan and Uncle Fred kept an eye out for hawks and humans, the mice marched into their room, department by department.

When everything had been cleaned out of the RV, the two humans set off in it to find the rental agency, and answer awkward questions about what was so wrong with this particular vehicle that made them need to change it?

There were only two things they could say, really. One was to claim that this massive beast was too big for their needs, which would have meant swapping it for a smaller one; and with 2,243 mice to carry, plus Trey and Julia, that wasn't such a great idea. So they went the other way, saying the RV was too small, because they hoped to pick up four more guys. Which would be true if Joey lost his game, and he and Jake and Larry and Curly flew out to join them, somewhere.

That made sense to the rental people, but they were still puzzled by the requirement that the new RV be of a different color. Who worries about color in a rental?

Before they drove back to the motel in the super-gigantic blue Mousemobile (instead of the simply gigantic silver one), Megan and Uncle Fred bought five pizzas: four plain cheese ones for the mice and another for the humans, with almost everything on it.

As they entered their room, meaning to cut the plain cheese pizzas into more than two thousand pieces, they were surprised to find the Big Cheese sitting on one of the beds waiting for them.

Megan noticed that the leader of the Mouse Nation sniffed the air appreciatively as the pizzas came in.

"Would you like a taste, sir?" she asked.

"Thank you, no," said the Big Cheese, as Trey translated. "A leader is never the first to leave a dangerous situation, nor should he eat before his followers are fed. Forgive me for the intrusion into your space, but I thought a conference was in order, just between us."

"Indeed," said Uncle Fred. "And maybe you can tell us about the man in the green truck. I mean, mice know everything. Right?"

The Big Cheese seemed to sag a bit. "Would it were true," he said. "But as you know, we have no special powers. No magic. We are limited to what our brains and our technology can provide us, and right now we have no clue."

"My first thought was that the man recognized me and Megan from that TV show," said Uncle Fred.

That brought the sign for "Smile" from the Big Cheese. "A fan, huh? Wanting your autograph perhaps? With all due respect, is it not more likely that our pursuer has some information about your role in Operation Cool It?"

"Wow. Cool It. That's a scary thought," said Uncle Fred. "Because you're so careful with that secret. We all are."

"Secrets leak, alas," said the Big Cheese. "So it is imperative that we track down this human to find out what he knows—and if he was the one who summoned the exterminators. Fortunately there is no hurry. Thanks to your driving skills, we can defer our research until we reestablish our Headquarters."

"In Cleveland?" asked Uncle Fred.

"Cleveland will serve admirably," said the Big Cheese. "Indeed, as your great bard might have written, in his play *Julius Caesar*: 'There is a tide in the affairs of mice, which, taken at the flood, leads on to Cleveland.'"

"Good old Shakespeare," said Uncle Fred, with a chuckle deep in his beard. "Always hits the nail on the head."

A messenger mouse had stuck his head around the door that led to the next room, and the Big Cheese waved him in. The mouse made an urgent gesture, something that looked a bit like swinging a baseball bat.

"Aha!" said the Big Cheese. "My friend here tells me that we may soon have information that will help us plan our movements. Come with me."

Uncle Fred held out an arm so the Big Cheese could climb onto his shoulder, and Megan carried the pizzas as they made their way into the mouse room.

A few mice looked up, and Megan could see noses rise in the air at the smell of hot cheese. But most of the mouse eyes were trained on the television set that the Engineering Department had connected to a Thumbtop that was streaming a game.

A Little League baseball game.

A game that meant one team could go on to the State Championship of Ohio and maybe the Great Lakes Regionals and maybe the World Series, and the other team would go home.

"Wow, I'm impressed," Uncle Fred began, as he sat down on the bed. "How did you . . ." But a few hundred paws made the sign for "Sh!" and Megan said it too, with a nudge to Uncle Fred's ribs for emphasis, because Joey was batting now, gazing intently at the pitcher, scowling in the way he did when he had to concentrate on a really difficult task.

And a hit! He got a single! The ball arched over the first baseman as a boy on third base slid home.

"That clutch single—it's what you expect from Joey Fisher," the commentator was saying. "He's tied the game! I bet the Cleveland coach would like a whole team of Fishers. Hey, look at his proud dad."

And there was a shot of Jake pumping his fists in the air, with a couple of wriggling bumps in his tall hat, if you knew where to look. Then, when the next batter came up and got a double that sent Joey around to score the go-ahead run, there was more joy in the bleachers. More wriggling in the hat.

"Pity Fisher can't pitch the last inning," said the commentator. "He's reached the official limit of pitches for the night."

And so it was that the second-best pitcher on Joey's team gave up a home run in the bottom of the inning with a guy on base, and it was all over. Just like that.

At first Megan felt deeply sorry, because how could you

not? This meant the season was over. No chance of a State Championship. No chance of the World Series. On the screen, she noticed that a couple of the younger boys on Joey's team had tears in their eyes, and a shot of the crowd showed a very quiet hat indeed.

But in that motel room, the floor, the bed, the dresser, and the top of the television set were one solid pirouette of mouse joy—until the Big Cheese made the sign that means "Freeze!" (you shake all over, as if you're very cold).

"Forgive us for our exuberance," he said, as Trey translated. "We understand that for the time being, Mr. Jake and Mr. Joey will be downhearted. But the predictions of our Director of Pastimes were correct. He had informed me that, given the lefty-righty matchup, defeat was probable. And I think you will agree that the addition of a second full-grown male to your team will be useful. We will therefore arrange for Mr. Jake and Mr. Joey to join us."

"But, sir," Uncle Fred began—just as his phone rang. "It's Jake," he said, peering down at it.

"Tell him you are arranging a flight so he may join us in Reno tomorrow," said the Big Cheese.

"I am?" said Uncle Fred. Then he clicked on his phone with a, "Yo, Jake!" as more than two thousand sets of eyes fixed themselves on his face. "Yes, we saw. Managed to get it online. Bummer."

Apparently, Jake's thoughts were so firmly on baseball that Uncle Fred couldn't get a word in, which was good, because while he was listening, the mice in the Transportation Department had time to make the reservation. A mouse with a Thumbtop on his back scooted over and turned around so Uncle Fred could read the information.

"Bet you want to know how things went for us," said Uncle Fred, peering down through his magnifying glass. "Short version: everything's hunky-dory. Long version: you're not going to believe this, but the mice had to leave Headquarters, so we've decided to load them all into an RV and drive them to Cleveland."

He held the phone away from his ear as it spluttered with laughter.

"I'm serious," said Uncle Fred, bringing the phone back to his ear. "And I need your help driving, so we've booked a flight that gets you to Reno tomorrow. Yes, Reno, Nevada. That Reno. From there we'll head east across the Rockies and . . ."

Megan thought she heard the phone say, "Rockies, huh?" And Uncle Fred made a thumbs-up sign to the watching mice as he listened some more, then gave Jake the flight and reservation numbers that would bring him and Joey to Reno.

"Didn't believe a word of it," he said, as he finally clicked his phone off. "Except for the bit about the Rockies. I guess he's hoping we'll drive home by way of Camp Green Stars, get to meet all those famous people."

"Can we?" asked Megan. "When we cross the Rockies, will it be the right part? Camp Green Stars?"

"Alas no," said the Big Cheese. "That is far to the north and would take us a long way from our route. However, as I would have told you this morning had not our meeting been interrupted, I do have good news about your parent. The clan at Camp Green Stars tells me that she is acquitting herself admirably, and has shown an ability to keep even the most succulent secrets of the stars to herself. You therefore have my permission to tell her the truth about our nation upon her return to Cleveland."

"Yay!" shouted Megan. She looked around to see if she'd startled the ranks of mice, but saw that they were all doing the sign for "Yay" too. (It's the left paw thrust into the air, once for a simple "Yes" and twice for something like a "Yay!")

And the paws kept on pumping twice, three times, four times, as Uncle Fred opened the lid of the first cheese pizza and started to carve it up.

chapter eleven

egan couldn't remember when she had last been so tired; though at least this was a friendly sort of tired, because Jake and Joey would be here tomorrow, and surely nothing more could go wrong.

Uncle Fred had decided to sleep in the RV. Normally, Megan might have tried out one of its seven beds too, but at this point of tiredness it seemed like way too much hassle. While Trey stayed on in the mouse room to hang out with some friends, Megan headed for bed in the connecting room, with Julia on her shoulder.

And saw that the room wasn't quite empty. There was a flash of pink on the bedside table, where she'd left her Thumbtop.

"What the . . . ?" she exclaimed, and felt Julia stiffen up. "Savannah?"

"Oh, hey there, girlfriend!" said Savannah, clicking at the Thumbtop like someone signing out in a hurry.

Julia leaped down and ran to the table, where she made some gestures to Savannah that looked distinctly frosty.

"Hey, don't have a cow!" said Savannah. "Can't a girl just check her e-mail in peace, without a few thousand mice looking over her shoulder? But don't you worry about a thing, honey-bun," she said. "It's all going to be just fine." And she jumped onto Megan's shoulder so that she could sing a few words right into her ear: "'Somewhere over the rainbow, way up high . . .'"

It sounded really bad, because no matter how hard they work at it, talking mice can't sing. Mouse brains and ears and mouths have simply not yet evolved to do music.

"What's going to be fine?" Megan asked, mostly to make the singing stop.

"That's my secret," said Savannah, and did a pirouette before she jumped down from Megan's shoulder and ran back to the mouse room.

Julia was making some signs. Pointing at the Thumbtop, then at herself, then making the question mark with her tail. Okay if she checked the computer to see what Savannah had been doing?

"I guess," said Megan, even though she really didn't approve, because Savannah might have been trying to set up a hot date or something—whatever mice did. But it didn't matter anyway, because without knowing Savannah's password, Julia couldn't find a thing.

During the night, the Transportation Department had studied the layout of the new Mousemobile online, and by morning they were ready to allocate a space to each department. It didn't take long for Megan and Uncle Fred to deliver boxfuls of mice to their allotted spaces, as Trey translated the instructions for who went where.

And what a difference a day makes. Yesterday, the mice might have indeed been robots, gazing straight ahead as they were loaded up. This time they were looking around and chatting, as excited as kids on a field trip; and a few even blew kisses to Megan as she gently lowered each box into place.

Almost last came the three talking mice, who were each given a cup holder to ride in, while Julia took the fourth. And last of all came the Big Cheese, who would again ride in the cage hung from the driver's mirror.

Megan helped by filling the kitty-litter trays and pushing them into the tiny bathroom. Then she filled some cereal bowls with mouse food and water. Sure, the mousekeeping crews could have done it themselves eventually, but for once they seemed glad of human help, glad to be with humans.

Uncle Fred was last to get in.

"Hi, guys," he said, turning around to look into the 2,243 pairs of eyes that were looking right back at him. "Can't wait to see how Jake and Joey react when they see you. Might even get a few EEEEKs out of them. No offense, sir."

That got a brisk comment from the Big Cheese, as Trey translated. "I know better than to take offense," he said. "Lamentable though it may be, I understand that, by and large, your species has an instinctive fear of ours. But not, I believe, Mr. Jake. He is, as you people say, one cool dude."

"You're right," said Uncle Fred, reaching up a hand toward the cage, where Megan was relieved to see a tiny paw stick out so Uncle Fred could tap it for a high five. "Way cool."

As the Mousemobile slowly pulled out of the motel parking lot, the Big Cheese gazed back at his subjects and gave them a cheerful-looking burst of MSL.

"Reno or bust," Trey translated. "Then Cleveland or bust."

And after Cleveland, what? Megan let her brain spin forward. They'd have to find somewhere for Headquarters, of course, probably on the second floor of Planet Mouse. Then in a week

or so she and Joey and Jake would head off to Oregon, maybe by way of Camp Green Stars. And she'd tell her mom. Finally!

With that thought, and the soft blue morning, the round hills the color of cornflakes behind them, and the great valley ahead—with all that, Megan couldn't help singing, and the song that came out was "Oh What a Beautiful Mornin'," which was what her mom would sing on the island when she stuck her head out of the cabin at dawn.

And everyone seemed to be sharing her mood, because when the Big Cheese said something that must have been, "Join in, everybody," a couple of thousand mice began making MSL signs in unison, silently singing along.

The only discordant note, figuratively and literally, came from the mouse Megan now felt running up her arm, and the sound of Savannah singing on her shoulder, just as badly as she had sung last night. Which might not have worried Megan much if Julia hadn't sprung from her cup holder and run up to the unoccupied shoulder, leaning forward to glare at Savannah under Megan's chin, her body stiff with jealousy.

Uncle Fred stopped the Mousemobile at a convenience store right beside the on-ramp to Highway 5—the road that would lead them to the giant Highway 80, which would in turn carry them eastward to Reno, then through the Rocky Mountains toward home.

"I smell doughnuts," said Uncle Fred. "Back in a minute."

And that was Megan's last happy thought for a while. Doughnuts.

It was a watch mouse at the back of the Mousemobile who gave the alarm. Peering through the crack that Uncle Fred had left at the bottom of the blind covering the rear window, he signaled something urgent to the Big Cheese, who stood in his cage watching, totally still.

Then, slowly and deliberately, he summoned Trey.

"What's going on?" asked Megan as she lifted him up to the cage.

"Nothing good," Trey whispered. Then he and the Big Cheese turned their backs while they communicated in the way of the modern mouse—tapping out words for each other on the Big Cheese's Thumbtop.

Uncle Fred was emerging from the convenience store with a paper sack in his hand and a doughnut already lodged in his mouth.

"'Ere's un 'or 'ou," he said, climbing into the Mousemobile. Then he took the doughnut out of his mouth as he handed over the bag. "One for you. And they had really cheap DVDs, so I bought one to entertain the troops. *Ratatouille!* How about that, guys?" he said, turning to look at the two thousand–plus pairs of mouse eyes that were fastened on him. "The world's best rodent movie, so as soon as I've finished my . . . What the . . . ?"

He'd spotted a flash of green in the sliver of parking lot that was all he could see through the back window. He checked his side-view mirror, and Megan did the same on her side. And saw it too.

The green truck with one fender in a lighter shade of green.

"It's him!" shouted Megan. "It's the man! The truck! Oh, sir!"

The Big Cheese was saying something in gestures that looked slow and sad.

"He knows," said Trey. "He saw."

Uncle Fred put his head down on the steering wheel.

"That means one thing," he said finally. "Some *mouse* must have told him where we spent the night. Some *mouse* must have told him we switched the old RV for this one."

That got the Big Cheese to the front of his cage, furious.

"It is indeed a major setback to our plans," he said, as Trey translated. "But don't be so quick to blame mice. If you compare our two species, you must agree that there is no record of a single mouse committing acts of treachery, whereas human history includes endless betrayals."

"But no way you can suspect me or Megan!" Uncle Fred almost shouted, sounding as angry as the Big Cheese.

"You are the only humans present," said the Big Cheese.

"It can't be us!" wailed Megan. "Why would we go to all this trouble and rescue your whole nation, then betray you? It doesn't make sense!"

"She's right," said Uncle Fred.

"We'll carry out an investigation later," said the Big Cheese. "For now, let us keep going as if we haven't seen that truck, as if we suspect nothing."

"But he'll follow," said Uncle Fred. "He'll follow us all the way to Reno. And when he finds out that we have a load of *rodents* on board . . ."

"Need I remind you," the Big Cheese said frostily, "that you are now under the control of rodents. You of all people should be aware of our power. I can assure you that if you follow my plan, we will extricate ourselves from this predicament."

"And still manage to meet Jake?" asked Uncle Fred.

"Of course we will meet Mr. Jake," said the Big Cheese. "He is one human we know we can trust."

Ouch! Trust Jake and not *them*?

Megan turned to look at the mice behind her, and, yes, she thought she could see suspicion in their eyes. It was so unfair! And Trey showed no sign of leaving the cage. On top of everything else, had the Big Cheese taken away her *mouse*? Her best friend?

She refused to look up at the cage, but kept her eyes on the road ahead, with glances at the mirror while the Mousemobile pulled onto the freeway, the green truck keeping its distance behind them.

Then there was a *plop* in her lap: Trey running up her arm to her ear.

"The boss is only pretending to suspect you!" he whispered. "He knows it must be some mouse, but if he makes everyone think you're the bad guys, that mouse will be more likely to take the next step. Maybe do something dumb."

"Can I tell Uncle Fred the Big Cheese knows it's not us?" she asked. "Look at him!"

Her uncle was bright red with rage, except for his knuckles, which were white as they gripped the wheel. "Not yet," said Trey. "Better let him stay really mad. The boss doesn't think he'd be good at faking it."

Which was probably true. What you saw with Uncle Fred was what you got: he could never fool anyone, even if he tried.

Megan just hoped that he wouldn't explode into a thousand pieces before they got to Reno. And Jake.

chapter twelve

After being so happy a few minutes ago that a song burst out of her, Megan now felt things were about as bad as they could be. She turned to see what was happening in the back of the RV, and that didn't help, because mice were glaring at her as if she were indeed the problem.

She glanced in her side mirror, and the truck was still there. Just behind them in the slow lane, then hanging back a bit to let a truck overtake it, as if it wanted to hide.

She remembered a scene in one of Uncle Fred's old movies. Wolves were chasing a horse-drawn sled across the snows of Russia. When the wolves seemed to be catching up, the people on the sled threw somebody off for the wolves to eat, so they stopped chasing. But no way mice would do that, would they? No way they'd throw her off for wolves to devour, wolves in a green truck? No, surely the Big Cheese wouldn't allow that, because he was secretly on her side. Wasn't he?

They'd been on Highway 5 for about six miles. Uncle Fred hadn't even finished his doughnut. Sick with worry, Megan hadn't even started hers, but maybe Julia would want some? She reached for the cup holder where Julia had been riding, but it was empty. Was Julia mad at her too? Could she possibly believe that *humans* were bringing danger on them all?

It was at this point that the Big Cheese came to the front of his cage and gave a series of commands that Megan didn't understand, except for the sign that meant "Thumbtop" (it's a pat on the left paw, where a thumb would be, followed by a tap on the head).

Turning to look for Julia, Megan saw that squads of muscle mice with toothpicks at the ready were swarming all over the Mousemobile, marching straight toward the Thumbtops at the heart of each department. No one put up any resistance, and in a couple of minutes, every Thumbtop in the Mousemobile had been pushed and pulled into a plastic container that the muscle mice had dragged from the kitchen into the middle of the floor.

Well, almost every Thumbtop.

Megan clutched her own tightly—until she felt a slight prick on her ankle from a toothpick, then feet climbing up her jeans. Three muscle mice appeared on her knee, with toothpicks in their mouths.

"Not mine!" she exclaimed. "You can't have mine."

"Not your what?" asked Uncle Fred, who'd seen nothing of the activity behind his seat. "EEEK! EEEEK!"

The EEEKs came when he felt something tugging at the pocket of his jeans and reached his hand down to check, only to feel mouse.

"They're confiscating all the Thumbtops," said Megan. "Ours too!"

"No way!" said Uncle Fred, driving with one hand while he kept the other clamped over his pocket. A muscle mouse on his shoulder gave a squeak, and as Megan craned her neck around to watch, she saw that he'd called for help. Five more mice with toothpicks came marching up the side of Uncle Fred's seat, while five started the climb up his jeans.

"Don't make us hurt you!" said the Big Cheese, as translated by Trey, who'd gone back to his post in the cage. "Just hand over your computer."

"The hell I will," said Uncle Fred.

Trey pretended not to hear. "And my leader wants your cell

phones too, please. Up here in the cage so I can answer if one of them rings."

"Uncle Fred, we have to," said Megan, because she could see that six muscle mice were in position to make serious holes in his neck. "Please!"

The "please" seemed to work, and Uncle Fred reluctantly fished his Thumbtop out of one pocket and his phone out of another and handed them to Megan, who lifted them up to the cage. She caught Trey's eye, and he gave her an apologetic little smile before reverting to his role as interpreter. The Big Cheese was giving a new set of instructions.

"Now no one can communicate our plans to the vehicle that I will henceforth refer to as Object X," he said. "And in a few minutes, Mr. Fred, you will take evasive action, similar to your maneuvers of yesterday."

"Oh?" said Uncle Fred. "Back roads all the way to Reno?"

"You do not need to know how we will reach our destination," said the Big Cheese. "Yesterday you invited me to make those decisions, remember? For the sake of efficiency, I suggest that you simply follow my directions. You will maintain your current speed for one mile and then you will slow down. . . ."

At this point Megan stopped listening, because she felt a mouse climbing onto her knee. A mouse with two dots on one ear. Julia. And Julia seemed frantic. She ran up to Megan's shoulder and leaned into her ear as if the sheer urgency of the situation might give her the power of speech—but all that came out was an anguished squeak, unlike any that Megan had heard from her before.

She lifted Julia down to her knee, where they could see each other, because with no Thumbtop for Julia to write on, they were reduced to MSL. But Julia was looking around nervously, as if she couldn't talk in public. Then she seemed to come to a decision, and made a sign Megan could understand. A beckoning. Come with me.

Julia took off, and Megan followed her into the tiny bathroom, where she closed the toilet lid and sat down, lifting Julia to the edge of the sink. But just being where they could talk without eavesdroppers didn't really help, because Megan still couldn't understand Julia's signs—until she made one that was unmistakable. She balanced on her hind legs and took a couple of wobbly steps—a sashay, almost—while at the same time she reached up a paw to tweak an imaginary something on her head.

"Savannah," said Megan.

Julia came back to all fours, nodding vigorously.

"What about Savannah?" asked Megan.

Julia quickly mimed tapping at a keyboard.

"She was using a Thumbtop," Megan translated, "before the guys took them away. Right?"

Nod.

"Could you see what she was writing?"

Julia drooped for a moment. Then a solution came to her, and she turned around to blow on the mirror, making a mouse-size cloud of mist.

"Got it," said Megan, and blew to make a larger patch of mist—one big enough for a mouse to write on with her paw. The letter *G*.

Megan blew a fresh cloud of mist for the next letter: *O*.

"Go?"

Julia nodded and made sweeping gestures with her front paws.

"Go away?" guessed Megan.

Vigorous nods.

"But who was she . . . ?" began Megan, but didn't need to finish, as Julia pointed to a green bottle of hand soap, then mimed holding on to a steering wheel.

"Oh, no!" said Megan, her *creep* alarm starting up big-time. "Savannah! So last night when she was using my Thumbtop . . . ? We must tell Trey!"

She tried to stand up, but at that moment Uncle Fred spun the Mousemobile off the freeway in such a sharp turn that Julia went flying and Megan was pressed against the wall hard enough to make it impossible to move.

When all four wheels were safely back on land, she lifted the bathroom blind just enough to see the freeway heading off without them, and with it Object X, the little green truck that hadn't been able to make the turn.

There was no way Megan could get back to her seat; no way she could tell Trey what Julia had seen, because the floor of the

Mousemobile was solid with mice, their ears and tails and feet tangled every which way so you couldn't tell where one body ended and another began. But surely Trey could come to *her*? Tiptoe over the top of the mouse morass?

"Hey, Trey!" she called. "There's something I have to tell you! Something important!"

Trey was standing on the back of the driver's seat. He did glance over at her briefly and gave her a wave, but he was busy translating directions from a geography mouse who was squatting beside him with a Thumbtop. Up one suburban street. Down another. Doubling back again and again, just in case. There was nothing Megan could do but wait until the mice on the floor had sorted themselves out.

"You okay?" asked Uncle Fred, when she finally got back to her seat.

"I'm fine," she said. Should she try to whisper in his ear? That she knew who might have betrayed them? That Julia had seen Savannah e-mailing, and guessed it must be to the green truck? But Uncle Fred was concentrating hard on following a route through the outskirts of Stockton, California, that no little green truck could have guessed at, even if it had managed to get off the freeway in time.

Megan decided to tell Trey instead, and leaned over to

whisper in his ear. "Something's come up. Something I want you to tell the Big Cheese."

"Not now!" he said. "Okay, Mr. Fred, left at the gas station."

Megan took matters into her own hands. She reached into the cup holder where Sir Quentin was riding, fished him out, and plonked him onto the back of the driver's seat.

"You take over," she said, then scooped up Trey and held him near her face.

"It's important," she whispered. "Julia saw Savannah e-mailing, and she's pretty sure it was to the guy in the green truck. And she was using my Thumbtop last night."

"No way!" said Trey. "*Savannah?* Why the . . . No way she'd . . ."

He looked stunned, and Megan remembered one day back in Cleveland when she and Joey were doing their best Sir Quentin imitation and Trey had gone very quiet.

"Don't take it personally, dude," Joey had said. "Just because you and Sir Quentin are such good friends!"

He'd meant it as a sort of joke, because no one poked more fun at Sir Quentin than Trey himself. But to their surprise, Trey had said, "Know what? We're not exactly friends, but when you're at the Talking Academy with someone for so long . . ."

"Sort of like your clan?" Megan had suggested.

"Sort of," said Trey, which meant that she and Joey could never make Sir Quentin jokes in his presence again. And with Savannah, it must have been the same deal, that tug of kinship that happens when mice grow up together. But this was much too important to let clan loyalties get in the way.

"Please, you *have* to tell the Big Cheese," she said. "You *have* to tell him what Julia saw."

At that moment, Sir Quentin had just instructed Uncle Fred to "Incorporate in your peregrinations a diversion in the direction of old Sol, that great orb that gives us warmth and light."

And Uncle Fred called out, "Trey! I need you. Please!"

Megan reached out to pluck Sir Quentin off the back of Uncle Fred's seat, and put Trey in his place, just in time to say, "Sir Q. means go east—take the next right."

Now what? Megan clasped her hands around Julia for comfort, and tried to think positive. At least Savannah couldn't do any more damage, could she, now that the Thumbtops had all been gathered up? And at least they'd meet up with Jake and Joey, quite soon. And Jake would fix everything—he'd make sure that humans and mice trusted each other again, wouldn't he? Because he was so good at that sort of thing? Much better than Uncle Fred, who was gripping the wheel as if he were trying to kill it, his anger almost sparking out of his beard.

chapter thirteen

"Could someone please tell me," Uncle Fred asked plaintively, "how we're getting to Reno? We just passed a sign. It's thataway!" He jerked his thumb to the right.

They'd rejoined Highway 5, now blessedly free of green trucks, and were heading due north.

"It should be obvious by now," said the Big Cheese, as Trey translated, "that Reno is no longer in our plans."

Of course. If Savannah had told the green truck where they'd spent the night, she probably told it about Reno too.

"Are you kidding?" exclaimed Uncle Fred, and for a dangerous moment took his hands off the wheel as he glared up at the cage. "What about Jake and Joey?" he asked, his voice rising quite high. "Do we just let them fend for themselves? Tell them to go home?"

"Absolutely not," said the Big Cheese. "When Mr. Jake lands, he will find a voice mail message that you will send when we reach the next rest area. Those directions will take him to the place where we will meet."

"And that place is . . . ?"

"To be on the safe side," said the Big Cheese, "I prefer to withhold that information from all but myself and my Director of Transportation."

"In other words," said Uncle Fred, "shut up and drive."

Megan gazed up at the cage, hoping to catch Trey's eye. Because when was he going to tell his boss? When was he going to let him know that all of this was Savannah's fault? She'd been watching Trey ever since they'd rejoined the freeway, and the Big Cheese had summoned him back to the cage. She'd expected Trey to immediately tap out a message about Savannah on his boss's Thumbtop. Or maybe just whisper the news into the Big Cheese's ear.

But nothing.

Was his loyalty to another talking mouse so strong that he'd never betray her? Even if it meant that the Big Cheese kept treating Megan and Uncle Fred as the guilty ones?

There was a stirring on her lap, and Julia gave her the quick jab that meant she had something to say. As Megan looked down, Julia pointed to her own eyes, then to Megan's, then shook her head, meaning "No." No what?

Megan became aware of the prickling behind her eyes and realized that she was close to crying, and that one tear had already leaked out. Julia was right. That would never do. You don't cry in the presence of mice unless you know those mice very, very well, because it's something they can't do, and it amazes them. The only thing that crying would get for Megan would be the undivided attention of 2,243 mice, fighting for positions where they could see her, staring at her in awe.

And the only way she could keep from crying, right now, was if Trey . . .

Julia took matters into her own paws and signaled that she'd like a lift up to the cage, where Megan watched her do something that mice simply don't, if they know what's good for them. She tapped the Big Cheese on the back. Then she pointed at his Thumbtop, where she quickly wrote something out. When she'd finished, the Big Cheese ordered Trey to read what she'd written, and Megan saw him slump.

The three mice clustered over the Thumbtop for a few minutes, writing messages to each other, then the Big Cheese came to the front of the cage and gazed at Megan before gesturing to Trey and Julia that they should both jump down.

They landed in her lap together, then each ran up one arm and climbed a braid so that they could dab at her eyes with their paws, because that's what they had done before when Megan cried, and it usually made her laugh, which, as they knew, was by far the best cure for leaky eyes.

But not this time. This situation was beyond laughter.

"Sorry, sorry, sorry," whispered Trey. "I really was going to tell the boss. It's just that . . . I guess I was in denial. Savannah was a great mouse when she was younger. She wasn't very smart, but she was so funny—until she started watching all those chick flicks. And then that's all she'd talk about. How she'd be a movie star herself one day, and wear amazing clothes. We told her there was no way, but she'd just say 'A mouse can dream.'"

Not for the first time, Megan felt glad that Trey had practiced talking with the sort of movies kids like—nothing to warp his brain, like the old historical dramas that made Sir Quentin yearn for past centuries, or the chick flicks that seemed to have addled Savannah's mind.

"So what did he say, the Big Cheese? When Julia told him what she saw?" Megan prompted.

Trey sighed. "He was really shocked. Then he said he didn't think she was in it alone. Doesn't think she's smart enough to have set it up herself, because she's, well, she's not the sharpest knife in the drawer."

Megan had had a competition with Joey once, in which they'd tried to think up the worst insults about each other's brain, so she had several dumb jokes at her fingertips.

"Missing a few buttons on her remote control?" she suggested. "A few peas short of a casserole?"

Trey didn't laugh. In fact he glared at her. Of course. He could say those things, but if you weren't a talking mouse, a member of his clan, he'd rather you didn't, at least in his presence.

"So who does the Big Cheese think is working with her?" she asked.

"He doesn't know," said Trey. "That's the thing. That's why he wants everyone to keep suspecting *you*—you and Mr. Fred. Just for now."

"But I'm worried about him," Megan said. She glanced at her uncle and didn't like what she saw. His face was way redder than usual, and a vein was throbbing on his temple. "He looks like he's going to explode, maybe have a stroke or something! I *have* to tell him!"

"Not yet," said Trey. "He might drive us into a tree. But we'll be stopping soon to send Jake that voice mail about where to meet us. You can tell him then."

It wasn't far to a rest area, where the Big Cheese instructed Uncle Fred to pull off the road.

"*Now* what?" he snarled as
he cut the engine. "EEEEK!"

Trey must have reported
Megan's concerns about her
uncle's health, because a
squad of five mice had started
on a journey up to his head,
and Megan recognized them at once as EMTs—Emergency
Mouse Technicians. Each wore a strip of white tape with a red
cross on it, crosses she'd made herself with a marker months
ago, at the request of the Big Cheese.

As she'd read on the Mouse Nation's Web site, most of the
EMT mice had specialized in mouse health, but a few had hung
out in human hospitals and doctors' offices, learning everything they could about the larger species.

"What the . . ." said Uncle Fred, as a mouse glued his ear to
the big artery in the neck that runs up to the brain.

"It's my fault, Uncle Fred," Megan confessed. "I told Trey I
was worried about you. But I didn't expect . . ."

She didn't expect, for instance, that mice would wriggle
inside her uncle's T-shirt to listen to his heart and lungs. It tickled, so Uncle Fred was actually laughing when a mouse stuck
his head out at the neck of the shirt and said something that

Trey translated as: "Three deep breaths, please, with your mouth open," and the mouse ducked back in to listen.

The whole examination only took a couple of minutes before the lead mouse, with a larger cross than the others, emerged to give his report. Without instruments, they could not be one hundred percent sure, but it seemed to them that the large human was in reasonable shape. He could continue to drive.

But first, of course, the little matter of the voice mail, the one that would give Jake a new flight number and destination. Uncle Fred reached up toward the cage for his phone, then started to go red again, because the Big Cheese kept a paw on it until a full squad of muscle mice had stationed themselves on Uncle Fred's shoulders, where they would monitor every word.

Uncle Fred climbed down and stormed over to a bench, as Megan ran after him and reached for his hand, which felt as hard and tense as a rock. How much could she say to calm him down, in front of the muscle mice, who had to keep thinking the humans were guilty? She couldn't use normal speech, of course, and whispering would probably bring on a major attack of toothpicks, which the mice looked very eager to use. And if she borrowed her uncle's phone and wrote a text on that, they'd be right there reading every word.

Then it came to her.

"Igpay Atinlay?" she asked.

"Esyay," said Uncle Fred, and Megan was glad to see the beginnings of a smile. "Though I'm not sure I can still do it. Been a while since fifth grade."

So she told him slowly and carefully in Pig Latin how Julia had seen Savannah writing to the little green pickup truck. And how Trey hadn't wanted to tell the Big Cheese at first because of his clan thing.

"The rat!" said Uncle Fred. "Ethay atray!"

"Otnay eallyray!" She spelled it out for him—how the Big Cheese was only pretending to suspect his humans, hoping to lull Avannahsay and any mice who were helping her into doing something really dumb. Umday. She thought of telling him some of the "she's so dumb" jokes she and Trey had come up with, but Uncle Fred looked as if he'd absorbed just about as much Pig Latin as he could, for now.

"Voice mail?" she reminded him.

Uncle Fred left his message for Jake and Joey, making it sound relaxed and cheerful and matter-of-fact, as if sending two humans on mysterious zigzags all over the western states was something that happened all the time. Yes, he said, he knew they would hate his news. Yes, he knew they'd both feel pretty beaten up after that heartbreaking loss and the early start this morning and the plane ride. Yes, he knew they'd be longing for a nice motel with a coffee shop and a pool. But there was just one more little leg to their journey. They should proceed to the counter of Southwest Airlines, where they would find a reservation in Jake's name. Here was the number. And when they got off *that* plane, there'd be further instructions. And no, Uncle Fred couldn't tell them where the plane would take them, because he didn't know himself. Wasn't that a hoot? They should think of it as a magical mystery tour, okay? A moustery tour. The sort of thing that happens when you hang out with mice.

"Oorpay uysgay," he said as he clicked off the phone and led Megan back to the Mousemobile.

Yes, poor Jake and Joey. But poor muscle mice too, when three of them climbed into the old birdcage to make their report to the Big Cheese. One of them started tapping on the Thumbtop with confidence at first, then looked at the others, who shrugged. A second mouse came forward and tapped out a few letters—maybe a Pig Latin word—but all it did was provoke the Big Cheese into making a short, sharp speech that must have been quite frosty, because the muscle mice looked as if they'd been whipped.

Now the Big Cheese had a word with Trey, and sent him down for a private chat with Megan.

"You really got them going with that secret language," he said. "They thought it might have been French. Or maybe Spanish. But Google Translate came up blank."

"Iay ontday alktay Renchfay oray Panishsay," said Megan.

She'd told him about Pig Latin one afternoon at the factory, when they'd finished their work and were waiting for the thunder of a fierce summer storm to stop crashing before they ran to the main house.

"Emay eithernay," he whispered, and turned around to shrug in the direction of the Big Cheese. If his boss interpreted the shrug as meaning, "It's no language known to man or mouse," that was fine.

The Big Cheese glared down in Megan's direction, but he did it with a wink.

chapter fourteen

What a difference a little Pig Latin makes! Now that Uncle Fred knew the plan, he calmed down completely, just remembering to glare up at the Big Cheese occasionally, as if the two of them were still mad at each other.

And the Big Cheese remembered to glare right back, for the benefit of his followers. Not that many of them noticed, because Megan had put *Ratatouille* into the Mousemobile's DVD, and the whole of Headquarters was watching, entranced.

Except for Talking Mouse Seven. Except for Savannah. Normally, the Big Cheese would have expected her to be right up front, maybe trying to steal some attention—maybe telling everyone she'd have been much better in the main part than Remy the Rat. But now she was quiet, not even looking at the screen but searching the faces of the mice around her.

Searching for what? For her posse? For the gang that had helped her make contact with Object X? For someone to tell her what would happen now, with no Thumbtop to write treacherous e-mails on?

But the truth about mice is this: they can't actually recognize each other until they get very, very close. That's why the Big Cheese always wore the fine chain that singled him out as the leader. That's why his directors wore a red thread around their necks. And plainly, the mice who'd been helping Talking Mouse Seven were determined to stay hidden, at least for now.

Which meant, of course, that the Big Cheese had to keep pretending to blame the humans. Had to keep remembering to glare.

The first showing of *Ratatouille* took the Mousemobile to the top of California's huge Central Valley. But one *Ratatouille* is never enough. Megan started it again for the long climb up through the mountains in the far north of California, and out the other side.

They were just half an hour into that second showing when Uncle Fred's phone rang in the Big Cheese's cage.

"Probably Jake—they must have just landed in Reno," said

Uncle Fred, looking at his watch. "You going to take it, Trey?"

"We're letting voice mail handle it," said Trey. "More secret that way."

Of course. Secret from the humans, who both remembered to glare up at the cage.

Fifteen minutes into the third showing of the movie, not far into Oregon, the cell phone rang again.

"Jake must have arrived," said Uncle Fred. "Wherever you sent him after Reno."

"This time I'll answer it," said Trey, and the humans strained their ears to hear his end of the conversation. Plainly, Jake was puzzled that he couldn't reach a human, because they heard Trey explain, "He's driving" and "She's sort of busy."

Then they heard Trey's instructions, which weren't yet the real instructions, because Jake would get those in a text within the next five minutes. Trey's voice went a little high and squeaky at this point, as if he were taking a lot of flak from the other end. Uncle Fred must have noticed, because he sang out, "Yo, Jake! It's complicated, man. Best do what Trey tells you, and we'll see you soon."

Where would that be, Megan wondered. At some point they'd have to turn right if they ever wanted to hit Cleveland. She strained to remember the Oregon geography that had been hammered into her head at school last year, when she was living with her dad in his little town of Greenfield. Were they heading for Portland? Because that was where the main Oregon mountains ended, wasn't it? A good place to turn east, toward Cleveland?

It was evening now, and they were still a long way from Portland—more than a hundred miles, according to the last road sign Megan had seen. So why had Trey reappeared on her uncle's shoulders to give directions? Why were they turning right?

And why did that old barn look familiar?

"It's Greenfield!" she shouted. She'd never approached the town from the south before, but once they were off the freeway, she knew this road inside out as the valley unfolded ahead of them, the hills behind it richly colored in the evening light.

"Are we staying here? Can we see my dad? Can we all go eat at his restaurant?" she found herself asking, then made herself look crushed by the Big Cheese's answer.

"Don't you understand?" Trey translated as loudly as he could, plainly intending that his words would carry to every mouse in the vehicle. "We're here principally to pick up Mr. Joey and Mr. Jake, and we are not, I repeat, NOT visiting friends and family. All contact with them is strictly forbidden, for obvious reasons."

. . . .

As the Mousemobile approached Greenfield, Megan sat sideways and leaned her face as far into the window as it would go, hoping to glimpse some friends or relatives, and ready to duck out of sight if she did. But the mice had chosen this route well, turning off the main road to skirt the southern edge of town. All Megan could see—and all that saw Megan—were trees and meadows and distant farms.

When Trey directed Uncle Fred to turn off the road, it was not toward the center of Greenfield, but away from it, heading deeper into the countryside to a barn big enough to hide a Mousemobile—big enough to swallow an entire nation.

It wasn't just the *size* of the barn that made it a perfect place to hide. It was the inhabitants. For some reason, the barn had become a gathering place for feral cats. Dozens of cats. So there was no way anyone on the Mousemobile could creep out at night to find a clan with a Thumbtop.

The cats weren't alone. In the middle of the barn stood Jake and Joey beside the Prius they'd rented at the Eugene airport, swatting at summer bugs above a carpet of cats rubbing against their legs. As the Mousemobile pulled slowly in, the cats must have detected the scent of massed mouse in the air, because they galloped toward it like kids seeing an ice-cream truck turn onto their street.

Megan unbuckled her seat belt and managed to slide out of her door without letting any cats slide in. She ran toward Joey and Jake, holding Julia high while cats leaped for her with soft yowls.

"Quick, in the car," said Jake, as Uncle Fred came lumbering after Megan.

When Megan climbed into the back seat, Julia wriggled from her grasp and jumped to the dashboard, where Curly and Larry had been sheltering from the cats. The three mice went into a joyous greeting huddle.

Megan felt the urge to go into a joyous greeting huddle with Jake and Joey too, but she wasn't sure how they would take it, so she made do with a huge grin at Joey in the back seat.

"Are we ever glad to see you!" she said. "We've had a hard day."

"You think *you've* had a hard day?" Joey said. "How about flying for about fifty hours without any real food?"

"Sorry about that," said Uncle Fred. "We can explain. Most of it, that is."

The comfort huddle on the dashboard ended, and Julia ran up Jake's arm to nuzzle him, while Curly did the same to Uncle Fred, then to Megan. Only Larry stayed on the dashboard, radiating sadness or sickness or something, looking almost like a mouse skin that was only half filled, floppy and heartbroken.

"Larry took it real hard," said Jake, reaching out to tickle him behind an ear. "That game. Much harder than we did. Hey, cheer up, big guy. It's not like it was your fault."

That was absolutely the wrong thing to say, apparently, because Larry sat upright just long enough to make the unmistakable signs for "Me bad" (you point the left paw at yourself and shake your head).

"Nice, Dad," said Joey. "Curly sent me an e-mail about it. Larry thinks it *was* his fault. He'd scouted the other team and he *knew* they'd get some hits off Sean unless he kept his pitches real low and inside. He thinks he should have gotten word to our bench somehow."

"Oh, come on, Larry!" said Jake. "Look, if Darren hadn't

been caught stealing, and if Frankie'd made that tag . . . Maybe Trey can cheer you up. Help you get things in perspective. Hey, where *is* Trey?"

"He's still in the . . . in that gas-guzzler," said Uncle Fred.

"Why on earth are you driving that thing, anyway?" asked Jake. "What, probably seven miles to the gallon? And why's Trey in there all alone?"

"Alone?" replied Uncle Fred with a short, barking sort of laugh. He swiveled to look at Megan.

"Shall we tell them?" he asked. "How lonely Trey is?"

Megan grinned. "Let's just show them."

Joey collected Curly and Larry, and Megan held Julia high as she led the way back through the leaping cats to the Mousemobile. Uncle Fred blocked off the door while Megan opened it and stood back so Joey and Jake could go in ahead of her.

And stifle EEEKs at the sight of more mice than they'd ever seen or imagined—more than the world had ever seen or imagined—in one vehicle.

"I told you!" said Uncle Fred. "Not my fault if you didn't believe me."

Actually the scene blew Megan's mind a bit too, because while the humans were in the Prius, the Big Cheese had set up a replica of the conference room at Headquarters—or as close as he could get, under the circumstances.

He was waiting on the Mousemobile's little dining table, with Sir Quentin at his side and the Mouse Council arranged in a semicircle around him. To their left was the Youth Chorus, which must have been busy with secret rehearsals on the long drive north.

Now, at a signal from the Big Cheese, the chorus lurched into song while Trey translated from his position on the back of the driver's seat:

> Jake and Joey, Joey and Jake
> Two whole planes you had to take.
> We're so glad to meet again.
> Baseball's loss is mousedom's gain.
> It's great that two is now made four
> And we cannot ask for more.

"You are indeed welcome," said the Big Cheese, as Sir Quentin translated. "Owing to the outcome of a certain human pastime, lamentable though that outcome may be, we can now benefit from the full measure of human assistance for our transcontinental peregrination."

At this point in a typical Sir Quentin paragraph, Megan

would have expected Trey to give a translation of the translation, but someone beat him to it. With a flash of pink ribbon, Savannah landed on Joey's shoulder and pushed her face against his neck in a mouse kiss.

"EEEEK!" said Joey.

"Sir Q. is saying like, you know, you lost a *game*?" she said. "Big deal, because it means you're here and we can be friends!"

But that was all she had time for before the inevitable roar from the Big Cheese, jumping high with each word as Sir Quentin translated: "Talking Mouse Seven will please descend from the human on whom she landed, immediately. Let us welcome our newcomers with whatever dignity we can muster in these unusual circumstances."

"Unusual circumstances indeed," said Jake. "Maybe you can tell us what's happening, sir? Like, to what do we owe this honor? And why Greenfield? Why not Reno?"

"After we were forced to evacuate Headquarters, we were being pursued," said the Big Cheese gravely. "For reasons that are unclear, and by humans about whom we know nothing. We have been betrayed. Whether by man or by mouse, we don't yet know, though I have my suspicions."

He glared at Uncle Fred.

"You can't mean . . ." said Jake, but Megan signaled "Hush," and he settled into a puzzled silence as the Big Cheese went on.

"Reno could no longer be in our plans, and Greenfield was chosen as an alternative meeting place because it is located at the base of a pass across the Cascade Range, which we will cross tomorrow. Furthermore, three of you are familiar with the environs, and can recommend an establishment where we might break bread together."

"Somewhere to eat *here*?" said Jake, putting his arm around Megan and giving her a hug. "There's only one place! Megan's dad runs the best restaurant in Oregon."

"We are, of course, familiar with that fact," said the Big Cheese.

Well, duh, thought Megan. Her dad's restaurant hadn't exactly become successful by accident: it had taken a ton of mouse-magic to change it from a failing French place called Chez Red, with very few customers, to Red Goes Green, where you had to book a table weeks ahead.

"However," the Big Cheese continued, "under the circumstances, it would be unwise to reveal your presence in this region. Any eating establishment must be selected with the assurance of concealment as the main priority."

"Sounds like it'll have to be takeout," said Jake. "How about that, Fred? You could go pick up a pizza or two, because no one around here knows you."

Joey had a better idea. "Hey, Dad, remember that barbecue restaurant in the forest? With tables way back in the trees?"

Jake ruffled Joey's hair. "Good thinking," he said. And to the Big Cheese: "It's a place where we can sit concealed in the deep woods, so there's no danger of being seen by anyone who knows me or the kids."

He unhooked the old birdcage and carefully made his way to the table where the Big Cheese and Sir Quentin were standing, flanked by the Mouse Council. "Here's your ride, sir— transportation to the restaurant."

The Big Cheese climbed into the cage. Sir Quentin was about to follow until Jake put his hand over the cage door, saying, "Sorry, Sir Q."

"Am I to understand," said Sir Quentin, "that you are specifically indicating that your humble servant is not invited to this repast? Even though I may assure you that my table manners are modeled on those practiced in some of the greatest houses of England?"

"'Fraid so," said Jake. "Another time. We'll bring you something good. But right now we only want your leader . . . and this guy."

He was almost out of the Mousemobile when he reached over to the back of the driver's seat and scooped up Trey.

chapter fifteen

t was Uncle Fred who drove the Prius, because he'd never been to Greenfield and no one would recognize him.

Jake had lived here all his life, more or less, so he sat slumped in the passenger seat with his baseball-watching hat pulled way down over his ears. Joey and Megan slumped too, staying as far from the back windows as they could, just in case anyone who knew them from Fairlawn Elementary School or Garfield Middle School was around.

As they drove, Uncle Fred started to explain why the Big Cheese had pretended to suspect his humans of the betrayal. But before he got properly into his story, there was agitation from the cage, and as they passed a row of streetlamps, Trey had enough light to read his boss's signs.

"Can we wait, please?" he asked. "My leader will have things to say about the events that brought us here, but for that he needs light."

So they talked about baseball as they skirted Greenfield and drove up into the woods on the other side, to the outdoor restaurant Joey had remembered. And, as he'd remembered, there were tables set deep enough into the woods for mice and humans to talk without bringing down a rain of EEEKs from other diners.

Uncle Fred took orders from everyone and fetched a heaping tray of human food, plus a spare hamburger bun and a slice of cheese for the five mice.

Make that four mice, because where was Larry?

"He wanted to be alone," said Joey. "I left him in the glove compartment of the RV. He'll be cool."

"So who's going to start?" asked Jake. "Who's going to tell me what's going on?"

Both Uncle Fred and the Big Cheese had just taken a bite, which meant that the Big Cheese could answer first, because with MSL it's no problem talking with your mouth full.

"It's complicated," he said, and Trey swallowed his piece of bun fast so he could interpret. "Some bad elements among my followers seem to have rebelled against my authority and concocted a plan that involved closing Headquarters down."

"How on earth could they do that?" asked Joey.

"Easy," said the Big Cheese. "Someone reported to the county authorities that Headquarters was infested."

"Wow," said Joey.

"It was really scary," said Megan. "The pest control guys came when we were bringing the mice out. We escaped just in time."

"Then," continued the Big Cheese, "we were followed."

"By *exterminators*?" asked Jake.

"No, by different humans," said Megan. She told him about the couple in the little green truck who'd acted like they knew her—and had turned up again in Tracy even after they'd switched Mousemobiles.

"But, but, but . . ." said Jake.

"But what do humans in a truck have to do with exterminators?" said the Big Cheese. "What's the connection? We don't yet know the details. But thanks to the sharp eyes of Cleveland Mouse 47—Julia, as you call her—we believe we know the identity of at least one rebel."

He made some more signs, and Megan guessed he was pinning the blame on Savannah—but guessed, too, that Trey couldn't bear to translate that part. And that the Big Cheese didn't make him do it.

"Wow," said Jake. "But why would anyone rebel, sir? I thought all mice loved their leaders and obeyed them at all times. I thought that was built in, part of their DNA."

"So did I," said the Big Cheese sadly. "It may be that contact with humans and human civilization has changed the mouse character. And that is indeed a sad and sobering thought."

"So what happens now?" asked Joey.

"Our present strategy is to lull the rebels into a state of complacency," said the Big Cheese. "Lull them into thinking that we blame Miss Megan and Mr. Fred, so they feel it is safe to make the next move. I expect those mice will soon reveal the goals of their rebellion, and the identity of any humans they have contacted. Then we can deal with that threat. But in the meantime, we have the principal rebel under close watch, so we can travel across this great land with no further surprises."

"To Cleveland?" asked Jake.

"Indeed," said the Big Cheese. "Tomorrow we will proceed eastward across the Cascades to the high desert of Oregon, then onward to the Rocky Mountains—"

"Rockies, huh?" interrupted Jake, leaning forward. "What part of the Rockies did you have in mind?"

The Big Cheese smiled, a paw pulling at each corner of his mouth. "Had we gone through Reno, we would have driven over a pass in southern Wyoming. From here, however, we will cross at a more northerly point, by way of a mountain pass not far from Camp Green Stars."

"And as long as we're in that neighborhood . . . ?" Jake prompted.

"As long as we're there, we can surely spare one afternoon for Miss Megan—for you all—to visit her parent."

"And, and, and?" said Jake, grinning now.

The Big Cheese made another sign for "Smile." "As I already told Miss Megan, her parent has proved herself worthy to be included in your little circle of Humans Who Know. Miss Megan has my permission to tell Ms. Susie the truth, whenever the time is ripe."

Megan couldn't help it. Couldn't stop her hand. Couldn't keep one finger from reaching out to tickle the Big Cheese behind the right ear. That was weird enough, because touching the leader of the Mouse Nation was something you never, ever did. But what was even weirder was the fact that her finger almost bumped into another finger, as Jake had reached out to tickle the leader of the Mouse Nation behind the left ear, while Julia, Curly, and Trey looked on in horror.

But the earth didn't open up, nor did the sky fall, and the stars kept marching across the night sky as they always had, and the leader of the Mouse Nation looked as if he didn't mind being tickled behind the ears, just this once. Didn't mind at all.

I could get used to this, he thought as Mr. Fred handed him

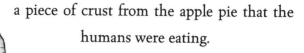

a piece of crust from the apple pie that the humans were eating.

A warm night. A moon just big enough to blacken the shadows of the forest. A million stars wheeling about overhead, the most stars he'd seen in years. The company of happy humans, humans he trusted to keep his nation safe. And hey, even that strange massage behind the ears had felt good. Yes, he could get used to this.

True, there was one sliver of thought in his head that was sounding a warning note. As Mr. Fred offered him a second piece of piecrust, that sliver grew. What if he *did* get used to this? What if he and his followers started to enjoy luxuries such as piecrust, and everyone began to seek them out? How long before the discipline of the Mouse Nation broke down?

He thrust that thought out of his head for now, because it wasn't going to happen. He wouldn't *let* it happen. He would be as firm as ever with himself and his followers. Just on this special night, this magical night in the forest, he had room for one more piece of piecrust.

chapter sixteen

t was getting late, and Joey had fallen asleep on the bench, his head on his dad's knee.

"I guess we'd better get back," said Uncle Fred. "See what your villains have been up to."

"There's no hurry," said the Big Cheese. "My villains aren't going anywhere, at least not tonight. Indeed, even if they managed to escape from the vehicle . . ."

He didn't need to finish, as the humans visualized the swirling cats. You couldn't have found any better jailers.

"In fact," the Big Cheese went on, "I believe we have time to take a slow route back to the barn. Few people will be about at this hour, and I have long wanted to view the historic sites of the earliest collaboration between our two species. Greenfield is, after all, a place of great significance to us."

"Yay!" said Megan. "And can we please start with the

restaurant? That was significant, wasn't it? The way mice helped my dad?"

So that was the first stop on the tour of Greenfield. When Megan had arrived last fall, her dad's restaurant had hardly any customers. Now, even late in the evening, the parking lot was stuffed with cars as diners lingered over their fresh-and-local desserts.

"Careful, Megan," warned Jake as they drove slowly by. He pulled his hat lower over his ears as the door of the restaurant opened and a happy band of people emerged. Megan ducked down low because many of the regular customers would probably remember that fifth grader with the red braids who'd often sat at the little table by the kitchen last fall and winter, doing her homework.

"Can I get out for just a minute?" she asked, when the people had driven away. She was feeling an almost magnetic pull to see her dad again. "Just to look through a window?"

But the most Uncle Fred would do was to take a slow turn through the parking lot, which gave them the briefest glimpse of the chef, some strands of red hair escaping below his tall white hat as he helped his staff clean up after a day of cooking. Of course Megan longed to burst out of the Prius and rush in and hurl herself at him, and of course she couldn't, but, as she told herself, she'd be here officially before long, and could hug her dad as much as she wanted.

When the Prius reached Joey's house, Uncle Fred parked a little way down the street, and all four humans tiptoed into the backyard, carrying the Big Cheese in his cage.

"Here's where I had to hold Joey's cat in a cardboard box while the big mouse raid was happening," whispered Megan. "While Trey was getting my Thumbtop back from Joey. Here's the cat flap where the mouse army went in."

The light was on in the kitchen, and with the curtains only partly drawn, they could see Jake's mom and Joey's grandma and Megan's stepmother's Aunt Em, all in the form of one old lady who sat watching television, a familiar orange cat on her knee.

Then the humans turned away to show the Big Cheese the window at the back of a house on the next street. The window of Megan's room.

To her surprise, the light was on, so she could look past the boughs of pine trees right into the room where she had spent so much time last year, gazing at the peeling brown wallpaper.

Except that the peeling brown wallpaper was now history. She could clearly see her stepmother, Annie, at work on the walls, in the huge shirt she wore for painting, a brush loaded

with blue paint in her hand. Megan felt so touched. Plainly, Annie was getting the house ready for her arrival, and wanted the room to look nice, finally.

The new paint was one more thing to add to Megan's good

mood as they all crept back to the car and pulled quietly away. In a couple of weeks, Annie would take her up to her room, and she would act surprised and pleased and hug Annie to thank her for the paint, and this time she'd feel really at home with Annie and her dad, not like last year when they were sort of strangers, and . . .

WHAM.

"What the—?" exclaimed Uncle Fred.

He had slammed on the brakes so hard that Megan's seat belt almost cut her in two. Trey and Julia each grabbed a braid to keep from flying, and the birdcage swung wildly.

"What the—?" echoed Joey.

Uncle Fred backed up the Prius so it was level with the lamppost that had freaked him out.

A flyer was stuck to it. A flyer with two faces—one of them very familiar.

Megan's face.

The photograph from the Web site of the Mouse Nation. The picture that had been pasted to the wall, low down, in almost every department at Headquarters.

And next to it a cartoon of a bearded man, the one Uncle Fred always used online because he was shy about letting people see an actual photo.

HAVE U SEEN SAVANNAH?

OR
FREDERICK BARNES?

Call me.

With a telephone number.

"You think . . ." began Uncle Fred. "You think Savannah is trying to pass herself off as *human*? Trying to pass herself off as *Megan*?"

"But how could it be Savannah?" Megan wailed, "when no one has Thumbtops? How could she have told anyone that we're here?"

"Good question," said Uncle Fred, then explained to Jake: "Every Thumbtop in the Mousemobile is under lock and key. Lock and toothpick."

"Indeed," began the Big Cheese. "We took care to . . ."

He was interrupted by a human sound he had never heard before. It was a wail from the back seat, almost a howl.

"Joey?" said Jake. "What's up?"

Another wail. Then Joey found his voice.

"I didn't know," he said. "I didn't know all the Thumbtops had to be locked up. I left mine with Larry."

"You left your . . . ?" began Uncle Fred.

"He wanted to follow a game," said Joey. "Little League. He said he could get it online. And I didn't know!"

There was silence in the Prius until the Big Cheese spoke.

"Do you know what we mice always say at times like this?" he asked, as Trey translated.

Even in her state of shock, Megan knew the answer. "It's, 'There is no disaster that mice can't turn to their advantage.' Right?"

"Right," said the Big Cheese.

"And the advantage here?" prompted Jake.

"The telephone number!" said the Big Cheese. "My operatives can easily trace the human who uses that number. Then we can instruct the mice in his house to find out everything about his goals and his plans and his contacts."

"First we have to take down all those damn flyers," said Jake. "Because if Red sees them . . ."

Megan imagined her dad finding his daughter's face plastered all over town. Of course he'd freak out. Of course he'd call the cops. Of course they'd send out an all points bulletin for Megan and Uncle Fred, one that would mean they'd be hunted in every corner of America. Find that girl and the bearded guy.

And if you find them, don't be surprised if you also find at least 2,243 mice.

No one talked much as Jake directed Uncle Fred to drive along the main streets of Greenfield, slowing as they passed a total of thirty-five lampposts that had flyers stuck to them, until Jake or Joey snatched them off.

At last they made it back to the Mousemobile, and Joey and

Jake sauntered over to it. While Jake shooed cats away, Joey carefully opened the passenger door. Then he reached into the glove compartment to scoop up Larry and the Thumbtop he'd been using, as if it were the most natural thing in the world that a boy would do for his mouse.

chapter seventeen

I guess you want to know what happened," said Larry as Trey translated.

Joey had placed Larry on the dashboard, where all eyes were upon him. "It was three–three in the fourth inning," he continued, "and then—"

"Hush," said Joey. "Larry, that's great, but hush. Your leader wants to know about something else."

Jake held out his hand to the cage and whispered, "Sir, be gentle with him" as he gave the Big Cheese a ride down to the dashboard.

The Big Cheese reached out a paw and patted Larry on the head to show that what was coming was nothing personal.

"Mouse," he said, "we believe that you allowed another mouse, or mice, to use Mr. Joey's Thumbtop."

"Was that a problem?" asked Larry, looking to Joey for guidance. "It was between innings."

"You couldn't have known it was a problem," said Joey.

"You couldn't have known," echoed the Big Cheese. "But somewhere on that vehicle, at least one mouse is reaching out to humans who wish us harm. Did anyone else use the computer?"

Larry crouched low, trying to make himself as small as possible.

"You can tell us," said Trey. "No one is blaming you."

"I thought it was okay!" wailed Larry. (You wail by ending your sentence with some quick pats on the right side of the mouth.) "It was that mouse with a bow, the talking mouse. She sort of rubbed against me as if she really liked me and said how big and strong I was, and she wanted to check her e-mail."

Larry put his face between his paws. Julia and Curly couldn't stand it and rushed over to stand beside him, glaring at the humans defiantly. If one member of their clan was in trouble, they were all three in trouble. They'd all three take the punishment.

"It's okay, big guy," said Trey, who, like Megan and Joey, had become deeply fond of Larry. Yes, he was a crazy sports nut—a sports bore, really—a one-track mouse, but there was not an evil hair on his body.

Larry ran along the dashboard to where Jake's hand was resting.

"Don't let them send me into exile!" he said. "Please—not exile!"

"There will be no exile," said the Big Cheese, "if you tell us everything."

"She looked at her e-mail," said Larry miserably. "Then she said 'uh-oh' or 'yikes' or something, as if she didn't like it."

"Did she reply?" asked the Big Cheese.

"Well, she wrote something."

"Was she alone?"

"She was, at first. Then after she'd signed out, another mouse came over. She whispered something to him."

"Do you have any idea who that was?" asked Trey.

"How should I know?" said Larry. "They all look alike. Except that this guy had a red thing around his neck."

"A director," said the Big Cheese, and his gestures were slow and sad. "A member of my trusted inner circle. I suspected as much, though I didn't want to believe it."

There was stillness in the Prius while everyone looked at him. He had plainly come to a decision.

"I need to send a message to my Director of Security," he said. "For obvious reasons, it will be safer to have a human deliver it. You will find him on guard, just inside the door. Tell him he is to bring the Director of Forward Planning and

Talking Mouse Seven to me, under guard. And please bring Mr. Joey's Thumbtop."

It was Jake who worked his way through the cats and used his body to block them out while he opened the door of the Mousemobile. The humans in the Prius watched as he reached in, turned on the interior light, then lifted up a mouse to whisper some instructions. He put the mouse back in the Mousemobile, then closed the door and waited, watching through the window. In less than two minutes he must have seen a signal, because he opened the door again, crouching down to let a platoon of muscle mice march up each arm. One platoon was using toothpicks to prod a mouse with a pink bow into walking ahead of them, while the other platoon shepherded a mouse with a red thread around his neck.

As Jake walked carefully back to the Prius, the cats went into a frenzy at the sight and smell of the banquet above them. There was no way any prisoner could jump down and make a run for it.

Nudging the cats away from the door with his feet, Jake lowered himself into the passenger seat of the car, and placed both hands on the dashboard so the muscle mice could march off, with their prisoners ahead of them.

"Why do you want to talk to me?" asked Savannah. "Do you

think Savannah's been naughty? Well, maybe I have, but that's all over now. I took care of it."

"We already know that you communicated with at least one human," said the Big Cheese while Trey translated. "Later we will find out *why* you did such a thing, but now we have more urgent questions. We must know who this human is, and why he is following us. And what does he know about our plans?"

Savannah looked at the Director of Forward Planning, who made a sad flapping gesture that Megan recognized as, "Go ahead."

"The man is called Kevin," said Savannah. "He and his wife, I guess they know . . ." She stopped and looked to the director for help, but he was avoiding her gaze.

"Go on!" said the Big Cheese.

"They know we have information, my friend and me. But we'll never never never give it to them, so you don't have to worry, they won't find out from us. Not a peep."

"Find out what?"

"Find out about Cool It!" she said, as if it were obvious. "Find out who's making those senators change their vote, things like that!"

And a dreadful stillness settled on the Big Cheese, the sort of stillness that warns mice an explosion is coming.

It was a controlled explosion. An explosion with small gestures, icy sharp.

And Trey translated it with short, sharp sentences. "You. Told. Humans. Something. About. Cool It."

"Oh, no no no no no," said Savannah. "Well, not really. They wanted to know, but we weren't going to tell them. Never never never."

The Big Cheese put his head between his paws. "But you got in touch with these humans," he said finally. "How could you? How could you violate our most important rule. The rule of CONTACT!" That last word came out in a roar, with a huge hop.

"It wasn't real contact," said Savannah, "And we didn't mean to. It was an accident! I can explain!"

"Explaining must wait," said the Big Cheese. "Open up your e-mail."

"But it's private, I don't . . . Ouch!"

A muscle mouse had given her a quick jab with his toothpick.

"Savannah," said Trey, putting a paw on her shoulder, "open your e-mail. It will be best for you."

She sighed and clicked onto Gmail, which mice don't normally use. She entered her screen name (Savtm7), and wrote in her password (Marilyn2) then turned the Thumbtop around for Trey to see.

"There are several messages from someone called Kevin," he said. "One came in last night, after we'd gotten away from the green truck the first time near Tracy." And he read:

> Hey there, Savannah, I guess your uncle really doesn't want you talking to me! That was some driving, getting off the road like that. We're still hoping to get your information, so we've e-mailed the license number of that RV to all our members in this area, and one of us will find you!

"And here's what Savannah replied," said Trey.

> Please go away. Don't you get it? I've changed my mind and I don't want to talk to you. And good luck hunting for that license number, because we're not even driving that thing anymore.

"See?" said Savannah. "I told him to get lost. I was *saving* you all. Like that girl in *Attack of the Blondes.*"

The Big Cheese cast his eyes up at the roof of the car and made a gesture that Megan guessed meant something like

"Aaaargh," following it up with, "You told him. You told him we'd switched to another vehicle!"

"I didn't really," said Savannah. "Did I?"

"I'm afraid so," said Trey. And he read the reply:

> Thanks for telling me about the switch! There aren't many places in this neck of the woods where you could have changed to a different RV, so it was easy to find the agency, and guess what—the guy gave me your uncle's name, and the name of your motel. I'll be right behind you when you set off tomorrow, still hoping for that information! Maybe my boss will double your reward, because your uncle is making it so hard for you to talk to us.

Next from Savannah came the short e-mail that Julia had seen her writing in the Mousemobile, just before all the Thumbtops were confiscated:

> Go away. I keep telling you. I don't want your crummy reward.

"See?" said Savannah. "I kept trying to get rid of him! Not my fault he didn't take the hint!"

She hadn't been able to check her e-mail again until the Mousemobile settled into the cat-filled barn, and she'd borrowed time from Larry. The message from Kevin that was waiting for her was the most chilling of all.

Trey read it out:

> So your uncle did it again, getting away from me near Stockton! But we're not giving up that easy. Your information is way too important, so we're still on your trail. We've got your uncle's name, remember? The researchers at our headquarters have found out some very interesting facts about him online. Like he has family connections in Greenfield, Oregon—so that's where we think you're at. Am I right?

"But look what I wrote back!" said Savannah proudly. Trey read her reply:

> That's just a lucky guess about Greenfield, and so what? It doesn't matter because by the time your dumb green truck gets here we'll be gone and you'll never ever find us.

"Which confirms," said the Big Cheese, stating the obvious, "that we're in Greenfield."

"So maybe it does," said Savannah, "but that doesn't matter, does it, because, like I said, by the time he—"

"Wait," Trey interrupted. "Another e-mail came in tonight. One you haven't read. It's from a different guy, somebody called Bud." He clicked on it and read:

> From: Bud9999@gmail.com
> To: Savtm7@gmail.com
> Subject: Hope to see you!
>
> I got your e-mail address from our headquarters, and they think you're right here in my town of Greenfield. What an honor! Please e-mail me so we can meet, or else I'll have to think of another way to find you.

"Bud," said Uncle Fred sadly, putting his head in his hands. "Looks like they're everywhere."

"And when you didn't reply to that e-mail," said Jake, unfurling one of the flyers, "Bud moved fast."

Savannah's jaw dropped, and for once she was speechless. Everyone was speechless until Megan broke the silence.

"Why *me*?" she asked, feeling a dangerous prickling at the back of her eyes. "Why did you give him *my* picture?"

Savannah looked at her as if the answer were obvious. "Well, I couldn't exactly tell him, could I?" she asked. "Tell him I was a *mouse*?"

There was silence again until the Big Cheese said, "Director of Forward Planning and Talking Mouse Seven, you will remain in custody while my legal team prepares the case against you. Tonight, we will study the rest of your correspondence with these humans, and, needless to say, I expect your full cooperation in telling us what you know about this . . . this hornets' nest you appear to have stirred up. Failure to reveal everything will result in the harshest of penalties."

He turned to the muscle mice.

"Change the director's status to suspended," he said. "So all may see his disgrace."

Two mice ran forward and pulled the red thread off the director's neck, then tied a knot in it and put it back.

"Now you may remove the prisoners," said the Big Cheese.

There was a cardboard box in the Prius, a leftover container from some fast food Jake and Joey had bought in Eugene. Jake held it against the dashboard so the muscle mice and their prisoners could climb in, then he carried it carefully over to the Mousemobile.

When he came back, the Big Cheese was bent over Larry

as he sat cowering in a corner of the dashboard, the picture of guilt and misery. And Trey translated as his boss said, "Mouse, there is no need for you to feel guilty! You did not harm our nation. Indeed, far from harming it, your actions—your generosity in sharing the computer—may, in the end, be of benefit to your nation, and to the planet."

Larry lifted up his head as if he didn't quite believe it.

"With the information we now have," said the Big Cheese, "we hope to find out everything we can about those humans as we drive through the night. We may even lure them into a nice soft trap."

Any other time, Jake might have laughed at the mention of nice soft traps, having fallen into one himself last year. But all he did now was reach out for a reassuring fist bump with the Big Cheese.

"Let's roll," he said.

chapter eighteen

e can move some mice," said Uncle Fred, when the humans climbed up into the Mousemobile. "Get you guys a couple of beds."

"Don't bother with that now, Uncle Fred," said Megan, thinking about who might be out there in the night, looking for them. "Can't we just get out of here?"

"Yeah, let's go," said Joey. "We'll sit at the table. These guys'll make room for us, right?"

The mice who had been allocated space on the dining-table benches scooted over to make room for the two kids, and those on the tabletop compressed themselves against the wall of the Mousemobile. They knew these young humans would soon need some empty table space in front of them, even if these young humans did not.

And soon after Uncle Fred and Jake had backed the vehicles out of the barn, and fastened the Prius to the back of the Mousemobile, and started the dark journey eastward over the pass, Joey indeed had his head down, asleep, with Curly and Larry nestled against his neck.

Megan could not sleep, with so many fears chasing each other through her head. Now she had more to be afraid of than just one weird guy in a green truck—now it was a big organization of weird guys with members everywhere, probably all looking for her, all with her picture.

Yes, that picture was already the most famous in the world among mice. But having it run loose among humans?

She needed to talk to Trey. If anyone could guess why Savannah had stirred up this "hornets' nest," as the Big Cheese called it, he was the one. But he was riding with the Big Cheese in the cage, both bent over a Thumbtop—maybe finding just what they needed to make this nightmare stop.

It was a reassuring sight, because mice can do anything, right? Before long, Megan's head went down on the table too, with Julia nestled softly against her neck.

It was a sudden stiffening of Julia's body that woke Megan. In the next second, she felt a mouse tapping against her cheek, and when she opened her eyes she saw a flash of pink ribbon in the dim morning light.

"I came to say I'm sorry," said Savannah. "So you'll forgive me."

With her head still on the table, Megan's eyes were about level with Savannah's, and, yes, Savannah looked as if she meant it. Or had she taken a class in "sincerity" for extra credit at the Talking Academy? Learned to slide into sincere-looking expressions at will?

Megan sat up. "Why should I forgive you?" she asked.

Savannah stroked her hand, which made it hard to stay mad, because a mouse-stroke is one of the better sensations any human can feel. "It didn't seem bad at the time," she said softly. "I just wanted a few nice things, like maybe some clothes. From the reward they promised. Just maybe a pink dress and a coat to go with it."

"But you stole my identity!" said Megan.

"Only because I didn't know you!" said Savannah, gazing up anxiously. "Like, I'd never met a human so it didn't seem important! It didn't seem real."

She took a step back for emphasis, and her tail brushed Joey's head, waking him up.

"Aren't you supposed to be in jail?" he asked.

Savannah sighed. "I *am* in jail," she said. "My *fur* is my jail.

No one can see the real me because of the way I look, trapped in the body of a mouse."

Joey laughed, but Megan couldn't help feeling a bit sorry for Savannah, who'd come out of the Talking Academy yearning to be a human. And not just any human, but one who was blond and beautiful and had closets full of clothes.

But showing sympathy wouldn't do, not now, when she could see hundreds of mice looking their way in the half light.

"You know what?" Megan said. "You're a mouse. Get over it."

For a moment Savannah looked so forlorn that Megan was tempted to tickle her behind the ears. Oh, why was it so hard to stay mad at mice? But she disciplined her hands, made sure they didn't reach out. And now she was saved by a squad of muscle mice climbing up to the table.

"Seems they don't want me to talk to anyone," said Savannah. "Don't have a cow!" she added as the first toothpick gave her a quick jab in the butt. "I'm coming, I'm coming."

She turned to follow the muscle mice, passing in front of Julia, who was making a gesture that Megan knew to be very rude indeed.

When Megan next woke up, it was fully light. The big Mousemobile had left the Cascade Range behind and was some way into the high desert beyond. Now it was turning off into the parking lot of a motel where the Big Cheese and his transportation team had booked a couple of connecting rooms at the back, well out of sight.

The humans kept watch for hawks while the mice marched into one of the rooms, with Savannah and the Director of Forward Planning in the middle of the column, hemmed in by a phalanx of muscle mice.

Trey rode Megan's shoulder into the human room, but he didn't stay.

"I'll be next door," he said. "That telephone number on the flyer was a great lead, and so were the e-mail addresses, but they need to question Savannah and that director some more. And I'd better be there."

"You don't think they'll *torture* her do you?"

"No no no, mice don't do that," he said. "At least I don't think so."

But he didn't sound very confident.

Megan gave him a pat and opened the connecting door for him. He walked through slowly, as if the mouse room was the last place on earth he wanted to be.

Jake fetched some breakfast from a nearby convenience store, but he and Uncle Fred were too tired to even finish theirs, so they crashed on beds while Megan and Joey changed into swimsuits and took their food out to the pool. After they'd eaten, they cannonballed into the water, splashing Curly, Larry, and Julia, who were sheltering from the sun under a towel draped over one of the poolside chairs.

Seldom had a pool felt so good, washing away all the dark fear and mouse dust of the night. They played a couple of rounds of Marco Polo, then met in the middle of the pool to talk.

"Savannah's so weird," Joey said, as they both treaded water. "What was she telling you in the night . . . that it was all for *clothes?*"

"Well, money for clothes. There was something about a reward, remember?"

"But she's a *mouse*. What's she going to do with money? Go to a mall with a bunch of dollar bills in her mouth?"

Megan giggled.

"Trey says she's not too smart," she said. "One twist short of a Slinky."

Joey remembered their old game, and Megan's giggles spread to him.

"A few fries short of a Happy Meal!" he said. "The cheese slid off the cracker! Only one oar in the water!"

Laughter engulfed him, and with one last gurgle of, "As smart as bait," he sank to the bottom of the pool and swam under Megan, then shot up behind her and splashed down.

"What's up with poor old Trey, anyway?" he asked. "He must realize Savannah's a dope, and sort of evil, but he still sticks with her."

"It's clan solidarity," Megan explained. "No matter what she's done, he can't help that clan thing. It's built in. When I told him Savannah had been e-mailing the people in the green truck, he didn't even want to tell the Big Cheese." She was glad her face was wet, because she could feel a tear or two coming out at the memory. "It was almost like we were on different sides."

"So he was a rat," said Joey. "A warthog."

Megan swung her arm to splash him. She was the only person who could call Trey a warthog—the word Trey himself preferred to "rat," because using a fellow rodent as an insult came too close to home.

"I was mad at him at the time," she admitted. "But now I'm sorry for him. That sort of loyalty, it's just the way mice are. It's in their DNA."

"Well, that bit of DNA must have skipped Savannah," said Joey, treading water more slowly. "The loyalty gene or whatever. One for all and all for mice. Hey, maybe they're still evolving, and Savannah just happens to be the first! And pretty soon they'll all be like her, wanting to live like humans. Wearing *clothes*. Like mice in kids' books."

That thought seemed to weigh on him so heavily that he sank again. Megan sank too, and they gazed at each other through the water, their hair floating up like red and dusty-yellow seaweed, their eyes wide at the new thought. Mouse evolution. A billion mice like Savannah, all wanting the finer things of life. Selling out their nation. Tearing up the treaty that promised mice would work with humans to save the planet.

chapter Nineteen

"If you were to define the middle of nowhere," Jake began, "would this be it?"

It was close to noon. Jake and Fred had finally emerged from their sleep to camp out in the shade of a big umbrella by the pool, with some sandwiches for the humans and crusts for the mice.

The middle of nowhere? True, wherever Megan looked she saw nowhere, more or less. The faintest humps of the Cascades behind them, dim in the heat haze. Maybe the fuzziest beginnings of the Rocky Mountains far ahead, with Camp Green Stars tucked away in one of the valleys, waiting for them to come by tomorrow.

"I wonder what Susie's doing right this minute?" mused Jake.

"Eating a soy burger, probably," said Uncle Fred. He never

seemed to get over the fact that his sister actually liked food that was good for her. "Organic."

"Is there any way we can let her know, d'you suppose?" asked Jake. "That we'll be dropping by?"

"Her phone doesn't work there, remember?" said Megan. "We'll just have to turn up."

"What, in that?" asked Uncle Fred, pointing over his shoulder at the Mousemobile. "You know what she'd say if she saw us roll up in that gas-guzzler?"

"She doesn't have to see it!" said Megan. "At least not at first. I've worked it out. We hide the Mousemobile in the woods or whatever. Then we drive to Green Stars in the Prius and take Mom for a walk, away from those movie stars, and I'll hold up Trey and say, 'Mom, Trey has something to tell you.'"

And how good would it feel to say that, finally? To know that her mom couldn't take it as a joke this time, couldn't think of it as yet another example of her daughter going mouse? She'd see Trey's lips moving. She'd feel his mouse heart beating under the warm mouse fur. Megan couldn't help doing a pirouette at the thought.

Sometimes she felt a bit guilty showing how glad she was to have a mom when Joey was around, because his own mom had been killed in a car crash when he was six. True, now that they lived so close to each other in Cleveland, Megan could "lend" Joey her mom from time to time, like when Susie went over to help him with his biology homework. Or they'd all go to a movie with Jake or on a picnic, which made Megan feel like they were more of a family. Except for that one problem: None of them could tell Susie the most important fact in their lives. Tell her the truth about mice.

Halfway through his second sandwich, Uncle Fred looked up.

"Mouse alert!"

A mouse with a piece missing from one ear was sprinting toward them over the hot concrete. Trey.

"Hey, you guys want to know what happened?" he asked. "How Savannah got us into this mess?"

"You better believe it," said Jake.

"Then be in our room at one o'clock," said Trey, and added with a sideways glance at Megan and Joey, still wet from the pool, "Wearing clothes. Okay?"

. . . .

187

On the dot of one o'clock, the four humans filed into the mouse room, wearing clothes. They picked their way to their designated seats on the end of the big bed, facing a desk where a number of mice were assembled, including one wearing a pink bow, and one with a knotted red thread around his neck.

But who were those other mice, Megan wondered—the twelve mice in an enclosure set off by pencils on the desktop? And that mouse sitting on a stack of sticky-note pads, with a piece of black cloth tied around his neck?

A judge, Megan realized. And that must be the jury—for a trial. But so soon? And what sort of trial? She wondered if it might be like the one in *Alice in Wonderland*, with upside-down logic and cries of "Off with their heads." But of course that was fantasy, and mice are nothing if not real.

"These legal guys know their stuff," whispered Trey. "The judge learned it when he hung out in the courthouse in San Jose—and the prosecutor too."

"Is there a lawyer for the defense?" asked Megan, remembering courtroom scenes from the movies.

"They didn't want one," said Trey. "Said they'd represent themselves, and besides, I guess there isn't much defense. The case looks solid. Wish me luck—I have to translate."

The judge banged his gavel—not that you could hear it,

because it consisted of an old piece of chewing gum stuck to a toothpick. But it worked, and all movement among the spectators stopped.

A bailiff mouse read out the charges from a Thumbtop at his feet, as Trey translated.

"Talking Mouse Seven and Director of Forward Planning, you are hereby accused of the high crime of plotting to betray your nation. How do you plead?"

"Guilty," said the director, using gestures almost too small to see.

"Guilty," said Savannah. "Like, I did it, but I can explain. I . . ."

Her voice trailed off as the judge gaveled for silence and signaled for the prosecution to begin.

The first witness was a mouse who had worked in the Department of Purchasing. The bailiff held out a copy of the Treaty Between Mice and Humans—his nation's most sacred document—and the witness briefly laid his paw on it before he used both paws to say in MSL, "I swear to tell the truth, the whole truth, and nothing but the truth."

"What happened on July twenty-seventh of this year?" asked the prosecutor.

"I was looking at a catalog of computer supplies online,"

said the mouse. "That mouse"—he pointed at Savannah—"came up and sort of leaned against me."

"And what did she say?"

"She wanted a favor," the mouse replied. "She wanted to look at doll clothes."

"Doll clothes!" repeated the prosecutor, gazing around at the assembled spectators to make sure the words had sunk in. "Clothes for human playthings! And then?"

"I told her that wasn't my job. But then my boss came by."

"Can you identify him?"

"That guy," said the witness, pointing at the slumped form of the director.

"The former Director of Purchasing," said the prosecutor. "And did he join the conversation?"

"You got it. He *ordered* me to find doll clothes online. I found some on Amazon.com, and that lady mouse saw a pink dress she wanted, kind of sparkly. My boss said, 'You'd look lovely in that gown, my dear, but I cannot order it for you. Our leader, the Chief Executive Mouse, would never allow it.'"

Megan glanced at the Big Cheese in his special place to one side of the court. He was looking straight ahead, completely still except for a twitch in his tail.

"And?" prompted the prosecutor.

"She said, 'Oh, he's so last century.' And my boss said, 'We'll do something to bring him 'round. We'll show him that a few luxuries won't hurt.' Next thing I know, we're ordering doll furniture. A whole bedroom set for the Chief Executive Mouse."

"And that worked really well," said the prosecutor, with the sort of sarcasm that lawyers often used in the courtrooms where he'd learned his craft.

"No, it didn't work well, actually," said the witness, a mouse with a literal mind. And he described how they'd set up the furniture in their leader's quarters—a bed, chairs, a couch, even a carpet. The Director of Purchasing and Talking Mouse Seven hovered nearby, expecting to be thanked. But when the Chief Executive Mouse saw the furniture, he went ballistic. He fired the Director of Purchasing right then and there, saying he couldn't be trusted with the nation's credit card, and would henceforth be known as the Director of Forward Planning.

"Was your boss happy with that title?" asked the prosecutor.

"He was not. He told us later, 'I'd like to tell our leader where he can put his Forward Planning.'"

"Like somewhere rude?" asked the prosecutor.

"Right," said the mouse. "Because it's not a real job, apparently. The Chief Executive Mouse does all the main planning himself. And my boss started talking about revenge."

"Well, how about that," said the prosecutor, pretending to be surprised and looking around the room as if to encourage everyone else to be surprised too. "Revenge. So your whole department switched to Forward Planning. And then?"

"Well, a day later Talking Mouse Seven came by, and she was very sad because she'd just read that memo, the one we all got?"

"The memo reminding us of our mouseness," said the prosecutor. "That memo?"

"Yes, that one. She said, 'Now he'll never let me get nice things.' But my boss said he'd thought of a way to get stuff for her, after all. You don't need a credit card, he said. An Amazon gift certificate would be just as good."

"An Amazon gift certificate!" repeated the prosecutor. "And he was to procure this how?"

"He didn't tell us," said the mouse.

"No further questions," said the prosecutor. He turned to the jury. "Ladies and gentlemen, as we shall now see, these mice were about to embark on a scheme that threatened the very fabric of our nation. To satisfy their need for revenge, to satisfy their greed, these mice were planning . . . CONTACT."

That word had a violent effect on the spectators. Contact had happened only three times in the history of the world: first with Miss Megan, then with Master Joey, and then with Mr.

Fred and Mr. Jake together. Contact was never to be attempted unless it was essential, and when it was essential, it required a huge amount of research and care. And these mice were planning to make contact with a human? Of their own choosing? Just like that? The spectators couldn't take it, and the motel floor became a storm-tossed sea of waving paws and ears and tails. When no amount of pounding with his gavel would restore order, the judge had no choice but to call for a brief recess.

chapter twenty

When the court reassembled, the prosecutor continued to lay out his case.

"I shall now show," he said, "that these two mice were not satisfied with making contact with any old human. Oh, dear me, no. They deliberately chose the worst of the worst—humans who hate us because we are so successful at educating the world about climate change."

That brought a gasp from the spectators (you gasp by opening your mouth and taking a step backward), and the judge gaveled for stillness before the next witness took the stand, a mouse who worked for Operation Cool It.

"And your job on Cool It is . . . ?" the prosecutor asked.

"I do opposition research," said the mouse.

"Which means?"

"I keep track of all the human organizations that say climate change is a hoax, or that it isn't happening, or that it's normal so there's nothing we can do about it."

"In other words, organizations that oppose our aims in Operation Cool It."

"You've got it."

"Did the director send you a request?" asked the prosecutor, as an e-mail was displayed on the big screen:

From: DFP@mousenet.org
To: Oppres8@mousenet.org
Subject: Climate Deniers

Could you please tell me which climate deniers
are most eager to stop Operation Cool It? I need it
for Forward Planning.

"Yeah, that's what he sent me," said the mouse.

"And you gave him the name of an organization?"

The mouse shrugged. "Hey, he's a director, so I had to. I told him about WATCH."

Another click and up came a Web site:

WATCH
We're Against the Climate Hoax

People, there's a secret organization right here in America that's trying to wreck our economy with false information about climate change.

Why is this group different from all those other losers who are saying the same thing?

Because they're effective! They've found a way to make two senators change their votes! They've silenced Bash Limpley, one of our most valiant voices in the media! They are the ones who are misleading millions of Americans.

Anyone with information on this shadowy group can earn a big reward!

"A reward," said the prosecutor. "For information about Operation Cool It."

He let those words hover for a moment in the deathly hush of the room. Then he continued.

"Believe it or not, the Director of Forward Planning and Talking Mouse Seven reached out to the leader of WATCH."

He waved, and the IT mouse brought up the next e-mail:

From: Savtm7@gmail.org
To: Jimbob@WATCH.org
Subject: The climate hoax

Dear Mr. Jim-Bob

I saw your Web site and I know who's making all
those people think climate change is real. I'll tell
you if you give me an Amazon gift certificate for
$100.

Savannah

The prosecutor let the silence run for a few moments before
he said, "Now, the leader of WATCH was obviously interested.
But he was cautious in his reply."

He waved a paw for the next e-mail:

From: Jimbob@watch.org
To: Savtm7@gmail.org
Subject: Re. The climate hoax

I am intrigued, but as I'm sure you will
understand, I'm not ready to enter into any deal
unless we can check you out face-to-face. Please
tell me where you live, and I can arrange for a
local member of WATCH to get in touch.

The prosecutor gave his audience plenty of time to read the e-mail, then he said, "Call the Director of Forward Planning."

The director shuffled forward and took the oath.

"Mr. Director," said the prosecutor, "what exactly was your intention when you and Talking Mouse Seven first contacted this human?"

"We weren't going to tell him anything about Cool It," said the director. "How could we? We're mice! Once we got the gift certificate we would have cut off communication completely. I know that's against human rules, but we thought this human deserved to be tricked. When he asked to meet us in person, I told Talking Mouse Seven, no way. I realized it had been a foolish idea all along, and we should break off contact immediately."

"And how did Talking Mouse Seven take your words?"

"She was mad at first," said the director. "But she saw my point."

"And the next time you saw her . . ."

"She wanted to show me an e-mail she'd written, though she wasn't going to send it. It was just to let off steam, she said. Sort of pretending we were in one of the movies she watched at the Talking Academy. Like *Blondes at Bay* she said. Or *Blondes Fight Back.*"

"No further questions," said the prosecutor. "Call Talking Mouse Seven."

Megan had half expected Savannah to frisk up to the witness stand, to sashay, but she walked on all fours like a normal mouse, her head low and sad.

The prosecutor took up the tale where the director had left it.

"Talking Mouse Seven, please read us that e-mail you drafted," he said, as a technology mouse brought it up on the big screen.

"Must I?" asked Savannah. "It makes me feel kind of dumb. It was just pretend, like I was in a movie? Like *Hostage Blondes*?"

"Read," said the prosecutor.

And Savannah did, in a voice so soft, Megan had to strain to hear it:

Alas, Jim-Bob! I am unable to meet you or your friends because of circumstances beyond my control. As you can see from my picture, I am a helpless young female. I am under the control of an uncle who might punish me severely if he knew I was reaching out to you. We call him the Big Cheese because he is the one in charge of the organization I was telling you about. He is the one who tells me secrets, like the truth about who got into Senator Court's apartment to eavesdrop on his conversations, and who forced that radio guy Bash Limpley to change his mind.

I wish I could tell you more in person, but I am not allowed out alone. And you would not want to visit me here, because we're in an old, old, old building behind Great America in Silicon Valley and it's full of MICE! So many mice that I sometimes think it is they who are holding me captive! I can see 32 of them right now and there are 36 in the room next door.

So farewell to you, Jim-Bob—I wish we could meet, but it is not to be.

Savannah

"So you attached the picture of Miss Megan, then you *saved* the letter to show your friend the director. Just to pretend you were living out a movie?"

"Right. It was just pretend."

"But?"

Savannah put her face down in her paws for a moment, then she looked up and said, "I hit 'send' instead of 'save,' Okay? But it was by mistake. I didn't mean to!"

And in the silence she lowered her head again, her shoulders shaking with the mouse equivalent of sobs.

After Savannah left the witness box, the rest of the prosecutor's case consisted of e-mails. First, a reply from Jim-Bob:

> Well, that was a surprise. I hadn't realized you're a
> little girl, and you are a very strange girl, if I may
> say so, but the important thing is that you're old
> enough to know that climate change is a hoax.
> And from your mention of Senator Court and Bash
> Limpley, I can tell that your information would be
> extremely valuable to our cause!
>   So here's the deal. If you can manage to
> go behind your uncle's back and give us that
> information, I am prepared to pay you double what
> you asked!
>   Two of our members live near Silicon Valley.
> They're a lovely couple, and you may see them
> in your neighborhood driving a small green truck.
> Kevin will e-mail you soon, and any time you are
> able to get away and talk to him, just say the
> word!

The prosecutor was plainly enjoying his role as storyteller.

"Our two prisoners ignored this message. And they ignored e-mails from this man Kevin. Indeed, they hoped they had seen the last of WATCH," he said, pacing up and down in front of the jury. "But Talking Mouse Seven had already said too much. Not just about her access to secrets that might earn WATCH hundreds of thousands of dollars from oil and coal companies. But about something else. Something that could help this Kevin find the building she was writing from. Do you know what that was?"

He paused and looked around the room, as if expecting a mouse to stick up a paw with the answer.

"Mice!" he said. "She told him about mice. That's when Kevin alerted county officials to what he called an 'infestation' in the neighborhood of Great America. The exterminators must have guessed that the building in question was ours. They did indeed arrange to visit our Headquarters. And Kevin must have been lurking nearby in his green truck, waiting to see who left the building. Waiting to follow."

The prosecutor spun around sharply to face the jury, one paw raised for attention.

"We shook him off!" he said. "Twice! But Talking Mouse Seven gave Kevin the clues he needed to keep following us!"

"I didn't mean to!" said Savannah.

"That is for the jury to decide," said the prosecutor, and for the next few minutes showed them the e-mails that had flown back and forth between Savannah and the green truck—the ones that accidentally told Kevin about the switch of a silver Mousemobile for a blue one, and accidentally confirmed that the new blue Mousemobile was indeed in Greenfield.

And when he'd finished, there was no sound except for that fake but sad mouse sobbing, the alternating chant of "boo" and "hoo" coming from behind the paws Savannah had pressed against her face.

chapter twenty-one

hen it was time for the jury to decide on the case, the twelve mice trooped into the human room to discuss their verdict in private. But not for long. In less than five minutes they were back.

Both guilty. Guilty of betraying their nation.

And the sentence? That would come later, when this long ride was over, when the Headquarters staff arrived at its final destination.

Trey stayed with Savannah in case she needed comfort, while the four humans retreated to their room to flop on beds and couches, exhausted.

They were all asleep when Trey came bustling in from the mouse room and ran from one human to the next, tweaking

hair and saying, "Wake up, wake up, and better straighten up this room a bit! The Big Cheese will be here in exactly three minutes. Very important meeting!"

And he did two pirouettes. Not just good news but very good news. "And if this works out well," he whispered to Megan, "it could help make Savannah's sentence a bit lighter."

In two and a half minutes, with the room halfway straightened, Joey opened the communicating door between the two rooms, and four mice came in—the Big Cheese, the Director of Geography, and two bearer mice, one with a Thumbtop strapped to his back, and the other dragging a cable that would plug it into the motel television set.

The Big Cheese was plainly in a very good mood.

"Change of plan," he said, and actually did a pirouette himself.

"Oh?" said Uncle Fred.

"While most of us were busy with the trial," said the Big Cheese, as Trey translated, "some of my best researchers were hard at work looking for the secret headquarters of this Jim-Bob and his WATCH organization. They were successful. So successful that . . . Let me put it this way. In a few days, or at most weeks, WATCH will be history. We can disarm it. Make it change its tune, before Jim-Bob has time to follow up on his knowledge about Mr. Fred—knowledge that could lead him to Planet Mouse and even Operation Cool It. Observe."

He waved a paw, and a mouse brought up a screen from Google Maps, showing a piece of the Rocky Mountains as seen from above, with snow-capped peaks, deep green forests, and two lighter-green valleys, side by side.

The mouse zoomed in on the northern valley so the humans could see what looked like a resort, with clusters of cabins on each side of a larger building.

"This valley," said the Big Cheese, with great satisfaction in his gestures, "is the headquarters of WATCH. Its beating heart. Here, a group of humans, funded by billionaires in the oil business, runs a Web site spreading misinformation about the unfortunate reality of climate change. There is a good road leading to that settlement, one that we can navigate with ease."

"Wait, wait, wait, wait, wait," said Uncle Fred. "You're suggesting that we should drive up into a valley full of humans who hate us? Who've probably all seen Megan's picture?"

"Have. Some. Faith," said the Big Cheese, with a pause between each word and a little hop at the end for emphasis. "We may be mice, but we are not dumb. Perhaps I should say, we are mice and *therefore* we are not dumb. To return to our plan, we will kill two cats with one stone. First, we will get those humans permanently off our tail, as it were. Second, we will persuade them to spread the *true* facts about climate change."

He looked at his humans, and it was plain to anyone who'd taken a course in Human Expressions (as all mice do) that the humans were having a hard time believing him.

"Have we not already changed the minds of many whose denial of the truth seemed unshakable?" asked the Big Cheese.

And it was true, of course—starting with those senators and that noisy talk-show host.

"As you will recall," said the Big Cheese, "the key to successful re-education has been the Thumbtop. It provides a constant connection between Headquarters and the mouse in the field, the mouse who knows best how to manipulate his human hosts. Unfortunately, there are some places where delivery of Thumbtops has proved virtually impossible, and this valley is one of them. Observe."

He waved for another view of the mountain and its two valleys, with the caption:

Thumbtop Distribution

There were three red dots on the town of Irving, just west of the mountain range. And another dot in the valley to the south of the WATCH settlement. But in the WATCH valley itself, nothing. And Megan could guess why. Normally, Thumbtop deliveries went to an empty house, or one whose owners were away, and mice crept out at night to retrieve it. Not so easy when there were no empty houses within miles.

"But what about *that* dot?" asked Jake, pointing to the southern valley, just across a ridge from the WATCH guys. "How did you get a Thumbtop in *there*?"

The Big Cheese paused to make sure everyone was watching him.

"That Thumbtop?" he asked. "That one was in Miss Susie's suitcase, although she didn't know it. That, my friends, is Camp Green Stars."

It was hard for the humans to keep their minds on WATCH once they knew about Green Stars; especially for Jake, who came out with some worried questions.

"Did you know about the WATCH people when you chose that site for Green Stars?" he asked. "If we'd known you were sending her . . . Megan's mom . . ."

The Big Cheese held up a paw to quiet him down.

"We did not know specifically who was in the next valley,"

he said. "But the two settlements are far enough apart. Their humans are not going to run into each other."

But Jake was on a roll. "Well, what if a couple of movie stars took a hike across that ridge?" He pointed to what looked like a trail leading from Green Stars over to the cluster of cabins in the next valley. "Then some WATCH guys followed them back to Green Stars?"

"Right," said Uncle Fred. "Even if all they did was tell the media about the camp, that would be the end of it. Photographers behind every rock! No movie star who's serious about the climate would go near it."

"Have no fear," said the Big Cheese. "I have seen the schedule, and the campers at Green Stars are far too busy for such hikes, so that does not concern us now. Our current task is simply to get a Thumbtop into the mouse community of this northernmost valley. Once we have done that," he said, turning to Megan, "you can finally welcome your parent into our little circle of Humans Who Know."

"Yay," shouted Megan, and did a pirouette.

Jake went one step further and actually did two pirouettes, the first Megan had ever seen from him. And they were not bad for a human—certainly better than her uncle's elephantine spins.

chapter twenty-two

They left early the next day, heading eastward across the high desert to the beckoning mountains.

Megan and Joey had grabbed a piece of prime real estate, the queen-size bed above the driver's cabin, where you could lie on your stomach and look out ahead to watch the Rockies draw ever closer and higher, even though the mountains didn't move fast enough for Megan, who wanted them here now.

Joey slept, and Megan was half asleep when someone grabbed one of her feet. She turned around to see Jake grinning at her.

"Bet you can't wait to see your mom," he said, waggling her foot.

"Right," she said.

"Me too," he said, with a wider grin than usual. "Or me

neither. Whatever. I think we've all missed her a lot. See any movie stars yet?"

Megan turned and gazed forward.

"Yeah," she said, pointing. "Rocky."

"Rocky Mountain or Rocky Stone?"

"Both," said Megan.

"That's so cool," said Jake. "Rocky Stone was great in *Hard Landing*, remember?"

Who could forget that movie, with Rocky Stone taking on a whole army of alien beings, his muscles rippling?

"And Daisy Dakota is there," said Megan. "Mom was so glad she's interested in the climate because every kid in America will do whatever she tells them."

Which was true. The Daisy Dakota phenomenon had swept through the land, making Daisy perhaps the most famous teenager of all time. And as if seeing Susie Miller in her natural habitat wasn't going to be great enough, meeting *Daisy*? Hey, she could probably have her picture taken with Daisy. Get her to sign it. Come away with something to prove to the kids in her class that she wasn't just a nerdy kid who was too old for braids and had a strange interest in the planet and mice.

She couldn't wait.

True, they had to call in at that other valley first, but that was just to drop off a Thumbtop. Right?

They passed the little town of Irving in its broad valley between massive peaks, and at a fork in the road a few miles farther east they swung left, on a road that wound up into the valley of the WATCH people. It was just as it had looked on the computer, with an excellent place to hide the Mousemobile behind a bluff where the road climbed high above a river.

Jake and Uncle Fred unhitched the Prius from the Mousemobile so it could take them the last few hundred yards to the old resort. At first Jake thought maybe Uncle Fred should stay behind, in case the WATCH guys had found a photo of him online, and whisked it from computer to computer along their network.

But Uncle Fred reassured him. He hated being photographed: hadn't allowed a single picture to get onto the Internet since his days as a football player for Ohio State, when he looked like a whole different human. He always hid behind a cartoon, which could be anyone.

But Megan—that was a different story, of course. Thanks to Savannah, her picture could be lurking on a dozen computers in that valley. So she had to stay behind—and Jake insisted that Joey should stay with her in the Mousemobile. Just in case.

Their plans were all ready. Plan A called for Jake to park the Prius close to the cabin nearest the road. If the cabin looked empty, Uncle Fred would carry Trey up to it and he'd give an urgent mouse-call, the high-pitched squeak that brings everyone running. Once local mice appeared, Trey would quickly explain what was going on, and Uncle Fred would hand over the Thumbtop and a solar blob to charge it.

If no mice showed up, there was always Plan B, which meant finding a safe place—any place—to hide a Thumbtop. Could be in a cabin or a hollow tree or a hole in a rock—anywhere the resident mice could find it after they read their e-mail, which they probably managed to do at night when the humans left their computers unguarded.

Either way, it shouldn't take long. With luck, Uncle Fred and Jake wouldn't run into any humans, but both men had cameras around their necks, in case. Just a couple of photographers looking for the best shot of the big snowy peak that loomed to the east.

Six or seven minutes, they reckoned it would take. Ten, tops.

Megan and Joey sat up front in the Mousemobile and tried not to look at the dashboard clock, which seemed to stretch each minute to about twice its normal length.

It was when the clock had staggered through five and a half minutes that there came a sound you hope you never hear when your uncle or your dad are delivering Thumbtops in territory that might be hostile.

The deep barking of dogs—large dogs that sounded enraged—followed by the distant shouts of humans. Then silence.

Megan and Joey looked at each other, and Megan tried not to show how scared she was. What if Uncle Fred and Jake never came back? What if she and Joey were stranded on the shoulder of a mountain in a huge Mousemobile that they couldn't drive even if they knew how, because their feet wouldn't reach the pedals? And you couldn't call the cops, when a couple of thousand mice on board had to remain a secret at all costs?

Savannah didn't help.

"Do you think that was Jim-Bob?" she asked, climbing onto Joey's shoulder, then leaping over to Megan's when he brushed her off.

Megan barely noticed what was going on as Julia, in full-attack mode with her ears back and teeth bared, raced up Megan's T-shirt to chase Savannah away—though she didn't go quietly. And Megan was vaguely aware of a spate of breathy words as Savannah told Julia that she, Julia, was just jealous of her because she, Savannah, could talk.

What now? Oh, why did *both* men have to go? Why couldn't one of them have stayed—an adult who'd know what to do?

The closest thing to an adult in the Mousemobile was the Big Cheese, so Megan turned to him.

"Should we go down there to see what's happened?" she asked.

"Absolutely not," said the Big Cheese, as Sir Quentin translated—and although the fact didn't click with Megan until much later, the situation must have been alarming enough to make Sir Quentin forget any extra syllables and talk straight. "At most," went his translation, "one of you could try to get a view of the valley, and report to me what you see."

"I'll go," said Joey.

"I'm coming too," said Megan, because just waiting did not seem like an option. "It's okay, sir," she reassured the Big Cheese. "We'll just go up to the top of this steep bit and look down. No one will see us. We'll be careful."

She wondered for a minute whether to take Julia with her, but looking at the bluff above the Mousemobile, she could see several places where the trees grew so close together that a mouse in a pocket might be squashed, or a mouse on a shoulder brushed off and sent tumbling down to the river below.

"Better if you guys stay here," she said, lifting Julia carefully onto the dashboard next to Curly and Larry, who'd been begging Joey for a ride.

"We'll be back soon," Joey whispered to them. "We're leaving you guys in charge, okay?" Then louder as he opened the door: "Back in a couple of minutes."

They climbed down. Just as the door was closing, there was a flash of pink, as Savannah leaped out onto Megan's shoulder.

"Like, I so want to see those humans?" she said. "After all they've put me through!"

Megan was tempted to pluck Savannah off her shoulder and hurl her back into the Mousemobile, but Joey had already started climbing up the slope, so she hurried after him.

It was quite a climb, steeper in parts than it had looked from below, and Megan and Joey had to pull themselves up by grabbing the trunks of the skinny trees that had found a foothold.

"Wheee!" said Savannah. "Isn't this fun? Just like in the movies! Real trees!"

Megan sort of wished a real tree would scrape Savannah off her shoulder, but she had enough on her mind to block out the excited twitterings of a mouse who'd never been close to a tree in her life.

Joey was a couple of trees above them, so he got the first look down at the settlement.

"Phew!" he said. "Looks okay. They're just talking."

As Megan scrambled up beside him, a huge wave of relief washed through her, and she even reached up to scratch Savannah behind the bow. Because this was how it had to be, if you thought about it. Uncle Fred and Jake had a great cover story. A pair of photographers looking for the best shots. And that shouldn't get you into trouble, should it? Here in America?

It was indeed a calm scene, almost as it must have been

when this valley was a thriving resort—except that when you looked closely, many of the cabins were boarded up, and the part around the main lodge that must once have been planted with flowers was now shaggy with weeds.

As Megan watched, Jake was pointing to the big snowy mountain, making a frame with his fingers as if he were asking about different views. One of the men was gesturing toward another part of the valley as he answered, and the big dogs that had barked so fiercely were now wagging their tails as they sniffed at Uncle Fred's jeans, detecting what? Doughnuts, maybe? Or mice?

"Do you think one of them is Jim-Bob?" came the breathy voice of Savannah from Megan's shoulder. "Oh, I'd so like to see him! Can we go a bit closer?"

"Savannah," said Joey. "There's no *way.*"

"Oh, phooey," she said, and was silent; and whether she was sulking or not, Megan didn't care, because the scene below was so much more important.

"How are they going to find a place for the Thumbtop, with those guys watching?" she wondered.

"Looks like they have a plan," said Joey. Uncle Fred had detached himself from the group and was heading toward the main lodge, with one of the men walking beside him.

"I guess Uncle Fred asked to use the bathroom," said Megan. "Maybe he'll leave the Thumbtop there. And look, there goes Jake!"

They could almost read Jake's thoughts as he said something that might have been: "I could use a bathroom too," because he and the second man also set off for the lodge. Plainly, Jake must have felt it was safer for the two men to stick together. After a couple of minutes, they were both inside.

"Oh, Jim-Bob, be nice to them!" called Savannah, not exactly shouting, because she didn't have the volume, but as loud as she could. "They won't hurt you!"

This was exactly what Megan did not need right now, and she sort of lost it. Forgetting caution—forgetting that they were in territory that was not friendly, to say the least—she yelled, "Savannah. Shut. Up."

"Hush," said Joey, who had seen danger. But it was too late.

"Savannah?" came a voice. Then louder, "Savannah! You're *Savannah!*"

chapter twenty-three

The boy looked about eight, with tangled blond hair flopping into his eyes, and shorts that were too big for him, kept up with a piece of rope.

As he came closer, Megan was terrified that Savannah might call out again, but she was blessedly silent, leaning against Megan's neck. Was she trembling? Had the prospect of real contact with a human made her think like a mouse, finally? At all events, she made no effort to speak as the boy took one last long look at Megan, then turned and ran, sprinting down the hill toward the old resort, his shouts of "It's that girl! It's Savannah!" getting fainter as he went.

"Catch him!" wailed Megan. "Stop him!"

"No way," said Joey. And indeed the boy was flying now, leaping from rock to rock with the ease of someone who knew that piece of mountain inside out.

"He'll tell his family," said Megan. "And they'll guess that Uncle Fred is the guy in the cartoon! They'll connect him to Cool It!"

They were paralyzed for a moment as the implication sank in.

"Maybe we should try to hike over to Green Stars?" suggested Megan. "Maybe take a geography mouse . . ."

"But those guys will come up here," said Joey. "When that kid tells them about us, they'll come straight up. And they'll find . . ."

Oh, just an RV stuffed with mice and their computers. Just the beating heart of the Mouse Nation. And here they came already: two men running out of the lodge and up toward the ridge.

Megan and Joey were stuck. Stuck because there was no way they could run back to the RV without having the men follow.

"We have to go down," said Joey, "to keep them from coming up here."

Megan nodded miserably.

And that's when Savannah took charge, because she was, after all, a mouse, and in times of danger, mice think really fast.

"You go on," she said, with none of the usual high breathiness in her voice. "I'll go back and tell the boss what's happened. He'll know what to do."

She took off alone down the cliff, back the way they'd come, back to her nation.

Megan was doing some of the quickest thinking of her life as she and Joey started down the hill to meet the men who were bounding up to meet them. What if she told them that she was Megan, she'd never heard of Savannah, and it must all be a case of mistaken identity—*stolen* identity? But then how could she explain why the four of them were snooping around here?

By the time the men were close enough to talk, she'd made up her mind. She put a hand on Joey's shoulder to slow him up and whispered, "I'm Savannah, okay? It'll be easier that way."

The men had stopped, and one of them turned and yelled down into the valley, "Danny was right. It's her!"

And as Megan and Joey reached them, he said, "Savannah, this is an unexpected pleasure! Did you decide to talk to us after all?" He swept off his baseball cap to reveal a bald head.

"And that man with the beard," said the other man, who had greasy hair down to his shoulders. "He's your uncle, right? The one who rented the RV? The one you called the Big Cheese?"

And it was a measure of the seriousness of the occasion, and the fear that had settled over them, that neither Megan nor Joey cracked a smile.

"I'll tell you everything," said Megan. But please, she thought, not yet. Not until she had time to think of what she could possibly say that would get them out of this valley. That would keep these humans away from the Mousemobile, and its cargo.

A man was waiting for them on the porch of the lodge, a man with vigorous white hair, his suspenders holding up jeans that sagged on the downward slope of a very large belly.

"It's Savannah all right, Jim-Bob!" Greasy-hair called out, "It's really her!"

"Savannah!" said Jim-Bob while they were still twenty yards away, spreading the name out in a deep voice that seemed to echo off the mountaintops. "This is an honor. As you must know, I've been hoping so much to meet you."

"My guess is her uncle and that other guy were spying on us, boss," said Baldy. "Spying on WATCH. And trying to get away with that cockamamy story about taking pictures."

"Savannah will tell us everything, won't you, young lady,"

said Jim-Bob. "What those men want, here in my valley. How deeply they are involved with that organization, the one that is doing so much to perpetrate the climate hoax. I think we can have some very interesting conversations, you and I."

Jim-Bob led them into the old dining room of the lodge, where several tables had been pushed together to make long desks that were covered with computers and printers and scanners and monitors. At the far end of the room were some comfortable chairs, though the two men sitting in them didn't look comfortable at all.

True, they weren't tied up or handcuffed. At first sight they could have been normal guests in a normal situation—if you didn't notice that men and a couple of women were blocking all the doors. Megan ran to Uncle Fred and wrapped her arms around his neck while she whispered, "I'm Savannah, okay?" And Joey must have whispered the same thing to his dad, because Jake said, "Hi, Savannah! I see you've met these nice men."

"Sit down, young lady, and make yourself comfortable," said Jim-Bob, his voice even more resonant indoors. "We may be here for a while."

He turned to Uncle Fred. "So you are the uncle," he said. "Well, maybe you don't know that your niece is smart beyond her years. She has seen through the fraud of climate change, and at one point offered to expose your efforts in that regard for what they are—a deliberate attempt to sabotage this country's economy. Am I right, Savannah?"

What could Megan say? That the person Jim-Bob should really be talking to was a *mouse*?

She mumbled, "Not exactly," but Jake was going along with Jim-Bob's scenario.

"Savannah told us everything," he said. "We've read all those e-mails, and trust me, she'll be punished. Grounded for life!" He laughed. "What an idea—trying to get an Amazon gift certificate out of you? I guess she wanted it for that new bike she's been clamoring for! But we were curious after we read those e-mails. We wanted to see what sort of setup you had here at WATCH. Very impressive, and now we've seen it, we'll be on our way."

He stood up as if this were a normal situation, and took a step toward the door.

"Not so fast!" said Jim-Bob, signaling to one of his men, who moved to block Jake's path. "Did you know you were trespassing on my property as soon as you left the road? And that I can make a citizen's arrest?"

He rubbed his hands and settled into a chair, as Jake sat down again. "You'd better get used to the idea that you may be here for a while—for just as long as it takes one of you to give me some information. Because something tells me this kid was telling the truth, and that you *do* know who's working behind the scenes to undermine some of our greatest senators. And some of our most fearless advocates for sanity in the media."

In the silence, Megan could hear the big clock on the wall ticking. No one moved.

"You're going to talk?" asked Jim-Bob. "Anyone?"

More silence.

"Tell you what, boss," said Baldy. "That RV? Gotta be parked up behind the bluff, because that's where we lost sight of it. Why don't I take a couple of guys and go search it?"

"An excellent idea," said Jim-Bob. Then, leaning forward as if he were sharing a secret, he said, "We have lookouts here, and saw you coming all the way up from the main road. Now, would you like to give me the keys to the RV? Or should my guys break in, to see what they can find?"

The four humans looked at each other with much the same thought: there was no way that could be allowed to happen.

"I'll talk to you," Megan found herself saying quickly, because that seemed to be the only way to keep everyone away from the Mousemobile. "But I'm awful hot. Could I have some water?"

"Forgive me," said Jim-Bob. "I was forgetting the rules of hospitality. Maisie! Water for our guests."

Three women had been hovering in a doorway, with the boy Danny leaning against one of them, beaming with pride. One of the women detached herself and came back with a tray bearing four glasses of water, the ice cubes clinking.

What now, wondered Megan. Should they throw the water in their captors' faces and run for it? But ice cubes against men with dogs—not a great matchup. So she used her water only to delay. Slow sips.

It could win them a few minutes, at least. But a few minutes until what?

chapter twenty-four

Savannah—the real Savannah—had imagined herself in many movie roles, but usually her imaginings were gentle and pink, to the sound of soft music. She'd never seen herself as a star in a movie where the future of her world was at stake.

It was Julia who later told Megan what happened in the Mousemobile after she and Joey took off. The first sign of trouble came with the shrill shout of the boy, and the distant yelling of men, and then the long silence, as the mice looked at each other and at the Big Cheese, who sat very still, waiting, listening.

Then a watch mouse gave a squeak and pointed at a pink blob hurtling toward them, sometimes falling, sometimes rolling for a few yards, sometimes bouncing off trees before taking another leap down the slope.

As Savannah came close, she grabbed one last sapling at the base of the hill and swung from it so she could land—*SPLAT*—on the windshield of the RV. There she clung to one of the wipers and managed to loop her ribbon over it so she was free to use paws and ears and tail for one of the most urgent MSL messages ever delivered: the news that all four humans were in the hands of the people who lived in this valley. People who recognized Miss Megan from her photograph.

At first Julia thought that it might be a trick, that Savannah might be lying about what she had seen. But just looking at her stuck on that windshield, with hawks circling above, Julia had to believe she was telling the truth, and it was clear that the Big Cheese took her news very seriously.

He was perfectly still for a moment. Then he summoned two directors to leap up into his cage and work with him on his Thumbtop. Julia could only guess what was happening from a sign or two—words like "Good trail" and "Urgent" and "Bring help." And yes, "Green Stars."

The Big Cheese closed his eyes, as if the step he was taking was indeed a momentous one, and made the sign for "Send." One of the directors clicked something—and all anyone could do now was wait. Wait and watch Savannah as she struggled to free her ribbon from the windshield wiper. But she was trapped because the ribbon was wedged tight between the blade of the wiper and its metal holder, and there wasn't a lot she could do but dangle and gaze upward at the circling hawks.

"The muscle mice wanted to rescue her, to bring her inside, but there was no way they could get out of the Mousemobile," Julia told Megan later. "We sat as close as we could, me and Curly and Larry, talking to her through the windshield, to calm her down. Savannah said, 'You hate me and you want those hawks to eat me,' and we said of course we didn't, she was a hero now. And then we started talking about doll clothes just to keep her mind off those hawks up there, though she didn't seem to take that stuff seriously anymore."

And who would, as hawks wheeled above, gazing down

at what should have been a delicious mouse snack, except for that pink frosting. What was up with that? Was it good for the hawks or bad for the hawks? And luckily for Savannah, they decided not to find out.

In the lodge, Trey was suffering from none of the paralysis of thought that was tormenting his humans. In times of danger, mice think with exceptional clarity. As soon as he realized that Megan was being brought into the building, he slid out of Uncle Fred's pocket and made his way to an empty room. There he gave the mouse-shout: a high-pitched call to action that humans can't hear.

It didn't take long for mice to come running. First, one or two cautious guys stuck their heads out of holes, then they gave their own squeaks to tell their friends and relatives that it was safe to emerge, and soon Trey had an army of about thirty mice—growing by the minute as word went out to the sub-clans in outlying cabins, who made their way cautiously toward the lodge.

When enough mice were assembled, Trey stood on a chair and explained in MSL what was happening. And as one of them told him, these mice could hardly wait to get their teeth into those humans. Normally mice grow fond of their host families over the years, but these guys knew about climate change and hated the way these humans were spreading lies about it.

In the next valley to the south, a mouse was guarding the Thumbtop that had been smuggled into Camp Green Stars in the toe of one of Miss Susie's shoes, then hidden under the dresser in her cabin. The mouse had been dozing through the morning, a little envious of the other members of his clan, who were all in the camp's lecture room listening to a talk about Greenland and what would happen if all its ice melted.

Then a soft beep told him an e-mail message had arrived. He couldn't believe what he read at first, but once he'd gone through it a second time, then a third, he realized this was much more than a one-mouse job. He ran to the lecture room, where his high-pitched call of alarm shook loose the twelve mice who'd been listening to the lecture from a hiding spot at the back.

Luckily, the humans were so focused on the speaker that no one noticed a dozen mice gathering near the door to make strange signs to each other before they took off in the direction of the camp office.

Luckily, too, the woman who worked in the camp office was at the lecture herself, so the mice were free to bring in their Thumbtop and print the instructions and the map that had been attached to the Big Cheese's e-mail. Then they formatted a message they could print on a sticky note. A message that read:

Megan needs help
more info
your cabin

They pulled the sticky note off the sheet of paper that had carried it through the printer, stuck it on the back of a messenger mouse, and watched him sprint for the lecture room.

Susie Miller was sitting in a chair quite near the door, so the messenger mouse didn't have to pass too many famous toes and risk any famous EEEKs. And it was easy to brush against Susie's flip-flops in a way that pulled the sticky note off his back. True, she gave out a soft squeak of surprise when she felt a note arriving on her foot, but the mouse had picked a time when the lecturer had just made an iceberg joke, and the audience was laughing, so no one heard. And no one noticed when Susie gasped at the note, slipped out of the room, and ran to her cabin, where she found two sheets of paper on her bed.

One was a map showing a trail that led up the valley for half a mile before diving left, up and over the shoulder of the mountain, and down into an old resort on the other side.

The other bit of paper told her what had happened—how Mr. Fred and Mr. Jake and Joey and Megan all seemed to be in the hands of the humans who ran the We're Against the Climate Hoax organization. She should come *now*. A Jeep could make the trek to the next valley in five minutes. And she should bring help.

That was all Susie needed, of course. Like any mother bear whose cub is in danger, she let instinct take over—not even pausing to wonder how messages had turned up on her foot, and then on her bed. She sprinted back to where the Greenland lecture was just breaking up, and grabbed Rocky Stone and two other famous action heroes, saying only, "My daughter . . . over there . . . the next valley . . . danger . . ."

That was enough—more than enough—and the action heroes ran with Susie to the camp's Jeep, passing Daisy Dakota, who begged to come too. The Jeep roared uphill, out of the camp, with Megan's mom in the passenger seat, one action hero driving, and two more squashed into the back with the most famous teenager in the world.

. . . .

Megan wished—oh how she wished—that the four Humans Who Knew had learned enough MSL to come up with a plan, under the eyes of their captors. As it was, with Jim-Bob's men standing around watching them like hawks, all they could do was think privately about ways to get out of this mess, which wasn't much use when they needed to act together.

As Megan sipped her water, she looked from Uncle Fred to Jake and back again. Was that the germ of an idea on her uncle's face, that slight raising of an eyebrow? She took the risk of going over to his chair, and buried her face on his shoulder as she whispered, "Any ideas?"

"Find Trey," he whispered back. "Say you have to go to the bathroom, and I bet he'll follow you in."

"Enough of that, young lady," said Jim-Bob.

"I just wanted to tell him I was sorry," she said. "Sorry I'll have to tell you some stuff. And I will tell you, but first, could I please use your bathroom?"

"Of course," said Jim-Bob. "Maisie! Take Savannah to the little girls' room."

The woman led Megan to the big ladies' room, then hung around by the row of sinks talking about how good it was that Savannah would help them undermine the efforts of those so-called climate scientists.

While she talked, Maisie was looking into a mirror to reorganize her hair, which she wore pinned to the back of her head in a bun. Luckily, it took so much of her attention that she didn't notice the mouse scurrying behind her, then under the door to a stall. A mouse with a piece missing from one ear.

"Oh, Trey," Megan whispered, as he ran up to her shoulder. She was so glad to see him, she was almost crying. "What do we do? How can we get out of here?"

"Easy-peasy," he whispered, and sounded like he meant it. "Here's the plan. There's a clock in that room, right? In three minutes—at eleven o'clock, straight up—do something to distract those guys. Like point out the window and yell. That's when we'll attack."

"Who will?" Megan asked.

"Me and the guys who live here. It's a big clan—at least fifty mice. And they *hate* their humans. We'll get them all EEEKing and squawking so bad, you guys can run for the car, then get that Mousemobile out of here."

"But what about you?"

"I'll try to come with you, but if I don't, no big deal. Just tell your uncle to leave the Thumbtop under the cushion of his chair. And I'll use it to set something up—I'll get out of here somehow."

"I'm not leaving you!"

"Megan!" Trey said sternly. "Listen to me. This is way more important than one mouse, and you know it."

And although mice usually can't scowl, he managed a small frown to show just how serious he was. He was right, of course. Every minute the Mousemobile was here, the whole nation was in danger.

"Okay," Megan whispered, giving him a last rub behind the ears. "Eleven o'clock."

She put him down on the floor, where he hid behind a canister of cleaner as Maisie finished with her hair, ended her monologue about evil scientists, and led Megan back into the big room, with its clock. Two minutes to eleven.

chapter twenty-five

s Megan sat down again in that big room, she wondered, did it show? That she had a plan now? She looked first at Uncle Fred, hoping he could tell from her expression that help was on the way, but there was no sign on his face or on Jake's that they'd guessed anything.

She didn't dare to go over to them, so she did the best she could in MSL—making it look like the sort of fidgeting you might expect from a kid who had to tell a really important story and was nervous about it. Both hands up against her head like big ears, meaning "Mouse." The word "Attack," which was sort of pecking motions—one hand on the other. Then one finger, twice, for "Eleven o'clock," and finally "Run," which she didn't know in MSL but made up on the spot, with fingers making a running motion.

And for Uncle Fred she signed, "Leave the Thumbtop in the

cushions," which was easy: a tap on the left thumb and another on her head for "Thumbtop" before she tucked an imaginary object under her own cushion.

Did her humans get it? Hard to tell, but plainly they realized something was up, and all three sat watching her intently as she glanced up at the clock.

A minute and a half to go.

"Okay, so let's have it," said Jim-Bob, rubbing his hands in anticipation. "Let's have the truth. Tell me how these guys keep trying to undermine our economy by faking up facts about the climate."

Megan took a deep breath and began a story, even though she had no idea how it would come out—and with any luck, it wouldn't have to.

It was hard, of course, because she had to make her story fit with the image of the Savannah these guys had in their heads—and get them to pay full attention to her so no one would be aware of any mouse-movement from a gathering army.

"It all began," she said, "when me and my mom were on an island in the Atlantic. St. Hilda, it was called. She was doing research on climate change and how it affects sheep."

"What's that got to do with the price of tea in China?" asked Greasy-hair.

"Huh?" said Megan, glad of any excuse to slow down. "I

don't think it has anything to do with the price of tea, or with China really, though China does have problems with pollution, doesn't it? Lots of greenhouse gas that warms up the planet. And it might have something to do with the price of *wool* in China because when sheep—"

"Hey, it's just a saying," said Greasy-hair.

"Then don't say it," said Jim-Bob. "Let's not interrupt Savannah while she's telling us her story."

A look at the clock. One minute to go.

"Well, my mom started to think that maybe the climate wasn't changing that much," said Megan, putting a hand behind her so no one could see she'd crossed her fingers to cover the huge lie. Of course, her mom had found the opposite—that on St. Hilda, at least, the climate was changing much faster than anyone had expected.

"Anyway, she didn't tell anyone," Megan went on, finding it easier to lie as she went along. "Except me, of course. Like, there wasn't really anyone else there for her to talk to, so she always told me everything. That was great, especially on those long evenings. We had this little cabin high up, where you could see the sea, but it was often foggy and rainy—"

"Is she going to get to the point?" asked Baldy. "Where's she going with this story?"

Megan looked at the clock again. Twenty-five seconds to get

through. It gave her an icy thought. What would happen if the mouse attack didn't happen, for some reason? And she just had to keep talking? Forever? Where *was* she going with this story? She had no clue, and crossed her fingers harder, then started talking again.

"As I was saying," she began, "me and my mom, we began to notice some things on this island."

There were the changes in rainfall, she told them. And the wind pattern. And then one day . . .

At that point, the big hand of the clock jerked forward and got to twelve. Taking a deep breath, Megan turned to the window and shouted, "Look!"

And of course all human heads swiveled to follow her pointing hand—and they stayed swiveled because, to Megan's huge surprise, there actually was something out there to look at.

A Jeep.

And in it was a very familiar-looking woman under a shock of springy fair hair, riding to the rescue with four of the most famous movie stars on the planet.

As Trey told Megan later, when he saw the Jeep, he thought of calling off the mouse attack, at least until he knew what would happen next. But there was no way he could rein in his army now. Some of the younger mice in particular had been longing for an excuse to take a bite or two, so they charged, and ran up legs, and leaped onto heads, and gave a few little nibbling bites to ears just to show who was boss—and it wasn't the four Humans Who Knew who sprinted out of the lodge first, but Jim-Bob and his followers, to the mixed sound of EEEKs and squawks and barking as the protector dogs went frantic in the room where they'd been locked up.

"Follow me!" yelled Jake, leaping out of his chair.

He led the way out to the porch, where a scene was unfolding that could have sold to *People* magazine for a million dollars. The three action heroes had rushed Jim-Bob's guys—the great Rocky Stone; Biff Morgan, who had the bluest eyes in Hollywood; and Nick Bender, who was kind of small in person but had been amazing in his last movie, where he took on a slew of bad guys single-handed.

Jim-Bob and his guys were so paralyzed by the combination of star power and mice that they surrendered without a whimper, as so many movie villains had done before them.

And here came Daisy Dakota walking calmly over to tell Megan, "I've heard so much about you!" and to give her a quick hug before

Megan's mom took over and hugged her as she'd never been hugged before.

The dust had settled. The action heroes had rounded up the men from WATCH and parked them in the old dining room of the resort, with their women and children behind them.

"Now what?" asked Uncle Fred. "What do we do with these guys?"

"How about calling the cops?" asked Rocky Stone. "They kidnapped you, didn't they?"

"Sort of," said Uncle Fred, "but if we tell the cops . . ."

Of course there was no way, although Uncle Fred couldn't spell it out. A sheriff and his deputies swarming all over this valley? Finding the Mousemobile? Luckily, Megan's mom thought cops were a bad idea too, because then there'd be newspaper stories with headlines about Green Stars, and their secret camp would be besieged by the media, with photographers hiding behind every tree.

"I think we can do something much more constructive," said Megan's mom. She turned to her four campers. "Guys," she said, "I've just thought of something for your final exam. I'll give you half an hour to prepare. Then you'll have half an hour to get these people to change their minds—get them to admit climate change is happening, and humans are doing it. Deal?"

"Deal," said Biff, the largest of the action heroes, rubbing his hands together. "Piece of cake."

"Way to go," came a whispered voice in Megan's ear. "If that doesn't kill two cats with one stone, I don't know what will."

Megan reached up to stroke Trey behind the ear. "You did good, mousie," she whispered.

"You weren't so bad yourself, kiddo," he whispered back, leaning against her neck.

Megan wanted desperately to get her mom alone, to take her on that walk she had imagined for so long—the one where she'd say, "Mom, Trey has something to tell you."

But that would have to wait, because everyone was busy now. The movie stars were in a huddle around the WATCH computers, planning their presentation, and Megan was helping her mom get the room ready—with Trey holding tight to a braid as if he never wanted to let go again.

"So, tell all," said Susie Miller as she and Megan each took one end of the table that the stars would use for their PowerPoint presentation. "And it had better be good. Here you are, turning up on my mountain unannounced, mixed up with some of the . . ." She lowered her voice so the clump of humanity in the middle of the room wouldn't hear. "Some of the weirdest of all the wingnut climate deniers. Did you get lost or what?"

"I guess so," said Megan, seizing on the one explanation that might just get her through this conversation. "Then Uncle Fred and Jake got talking to these guys. . . . We were going to come to Green Stars, but Uncle Fred and Jake . . . It's all complicated."

"But why did Fred bring you out west at all?" asked her mom. "Were you on your way to your dad a bit early? *Driving to Oregon?* That might have made sense in a Prius or something, but in that huge gas-guzzler? We passed it on the way—I knew it must have something to do with you, because of that toy mouse that was dangling on the windshield. But really . . ."

A mouse dangling on the windshield? A toy mouse? Could that mean a *dead* mouse? Megan remembered her last look at Savannah, bounding off through the trees, a sudden hero in a pink ribbon. It had to be Savannah dangling. But alive or dead? Someone had to get up there as soon as possible, which meant getting rid of her mom right now, ending the flow of questions.

As if he could read her mind, Trey whispered, "Tell her it was all Jake's idea to come here. Get her to go ask him!"

"It was Jake's idea," Megan said. "Jake realized that Green Stars was on our way, like halfway between Cleveland and Greenfield. And he said—"

"It was *Jake's* idea?" her mom interrupted.

Megan shrugged. "Why don't you ask him about it?" she suggested, and that worked fine. Her mom walked off in the direction of Jake, and Megan could slip away to check on that mouse on the windshield.

With Trey hanging on to a braid, she raced back the way she and Joey had come, up the steep slope to the bluff above the river. It felt much steeper this time, and Megan had to stop a couple of times to catch her breath. In fact, she barely had enough breath left to tell Trey about Savannah—how she'd gone back alone to sound the alarm.

"Even though she's . . ." Trey began.

"No!" said Megan. "No more Savannah jokes."

"I was only going to say, even though she's hardly ever been outdoors before," said Trey. "Probably never even seen a tree. That's one brave mouse."

Megan reached up and tickled him behind the ear to apologize for having suspected even for a second that he'd come out with a dumb joke at a time like this.

At last she reached the top of the bluff and skidded as fast as she could down the other side, grabbing young trees to slow her progress.

And yes, there was the mouse. And yes, it looked lifeless, dangling, caught on the windshield wiper. It couldn't be dead. *Please, please, please,* Megan thought as she bounced off the last tree. *Let Savannah not be dead.*

chapter twenty-fix

egan leaned against the front of the Mousemobile and gazed upward. Behind the windshield, she could see the anxious faces of Curly, Larry, and Julia gazing down. And in front of them, caught on the windshield, the limp blob of Savannah dangling from her pink ribbon.

Megan stretched up to free her, but the Mousemobile had been parked with its front wheels on a slight rise, and even on tiptoe, Megan found she simply couldn't reach the windshield. She was about to turn away to look for a stick she might use to bend the windshield wiper toward her when a man's hand appeared over her head and plucked Savannah down.

Jake.

And at just the right moment, or the wrong moment,

depending on your point of view, Susie Miller ran toward the Mousemobile from the Prius that had brought her and Jake up from the valley. She'd panicked when she saw her daughter heading off alone into territory that could still be hostile. With her mother bear instincts at full pitch, she'd begged Jake to drive her as fast as he could to the big old gas-guzzler, which was where Megan seemed to be heading. And now here she was, rushing up to hug Megan just as the mouse in Jake's hand sat up and started to sing: "'Someday, my prince will come. Someday we'll meet again.'"

It didn't sound great, because when you can't sing anyway, then spend much of the afternoon on a windshield as hawk bait, it's *never* going to sound great, but it had an effect. Susie Miller pretty much fainted. Luckily, she couldn't faint far: the mossy bank of the steep bluff caught her softly, almost upright. And she didn't pass all the way out, so while Jake squeezed one of her hands and Megan squeezed the other, she half opened her eyes and said, "Not a great time for a stunt like that, kiddo— singing like a mouse. My nerves are already . . . What's *that* mouse doing?"

Megan looked around to follow her mom's gaze and saw that the Big Cheese, still in his cage, was deep into an elaborate-looking speech.

"I don't know what those signs mean," Megan said truthfully. She looked at Trey, hoping he would whisper the translation into her ear.

But he went further than that, and hopped off her shoulder to sit on the bank near Susie, gazing up into her face.

"Yay!" he said, as loudly as he could. "It's so cool! That's my boss in there, and he has a message for you. You are the fifth human to learn that mice have evolved. Welcome to our world!"

"YESSS!" yelled Jake at the top of his voice, laughing as

Megan hurled herself at her mom, saying, "Now you know! Now I can I tell you everything!"

No, Susie didn't faint again, but she did lie back against the mossy bank with her eyes shut.

"It's been so hard," Jake was saying. "Not being able to tell you about mice—not just hard on Megan, but all four of us."

"You do know, don't you," said Susie, slowly and carefully, her eyes still shut, "that evolution is an incredibly slow process. So, Megan, that mouse of yours wasn't really talking. No way. Even if mice had the brain capacity to process language, which they do not, it would be scientifically impossible for them to make the sounds."

It was Trey who answered her.

"Not being a scientist myself," he said, "I would normally defer to your greater knowledge. But in this case I have to disagree because, as you'd see if you would only open your eyes, I am a mouse, and I am talking. True, not many of us can make human sounds. I and my brave colleague here"—he waved at Savannah—"are rare in that respect. But we can all *think*. And use computers. And communicate."

Susie opened one eye and looked at him for a moment as

he gave her a loopy grin, the one he'd learned for extra credit in his Human Expressions class.

"Fred," Susie said.

"Huh?" said Megan.

"It's Fred. He finally came up with a good invention. Really convincing robot mice. Probably remote controlled."

She turned her gaze on the windshield, where several excited mice were talking all at once in MSL, as if they might indeed be robots. "See?" said Susie.

"Here we go again," said Trey. "I went through this with Megan last year, and then with Joey, then with Mr. Fred and Mr. Jake."

He climbed down the bank to where Susie's hand was resting.

"Haaaaaaaaa," he said, leaning over to blow on it gently. "Warm breath, right? Mouse breath. Not robot breath." He flattened himself against the back of her hand so she could feel as much of his body as possible. "Warm body. Mouse body. Not a robot with central heating."

It took a few minutes for Susie Miller's scientific brain to agree with her regular brain. And when it did, she had a hundred questions, of course, about how mice evolved, and where, and when.

Trey quickly ran through the main facts—how some mice had spent so much time watching young geeks in Silicon Valley that they learned how to use computers themselves. And how—once they could use language—they found out how smart they really were.

Susie put her hands over her face as if it was all too much to take in—but when she took her hands away she was laughing. "Planet Mouse, in Cleveland," she said. "Do you mean to tell me you have real *mice* working in there?"

"Of course we do," said Jake. "Making Thumbtops. Thumbtops and blobs, just like our sign says."

"The Thumbtops are mostly for mice," explained Megan, "so they can stop climate change."

"Whoa!" said her mom, pushing herself upright. "So they can stop *what*? Holy cow! Mice?"

"Why not?" said Megan. "They want to help the planet as much as we do."

"So when I was giving Freddy credit for turning green . . ."

"He's really committed to that now," said Jake. "But it started with mice."

"And you couldn't tell me any of this, Megan? You've known about mice for months and months and you couldn't tell your own *mother*?"

"I wanted to," said Megan. "I wanted to so much. But he said you weren't ready."

"He?"

"The big guy," said Jake.

With Savannah still resting in his left hand, Jake used the other one to unlock the door of the Mousemobile and bring out the Big Cheese in his cage.

"This is our leader," said Trey, as the Big Cheese went into a speech. "The Chief Executive Mouse. He'd like to address you in human speech, but he doesn't have the right sort of mouth, so I will translate. He's saying, 'We bid you welcome, Miss Susie. Now is probably not the time to explain how I and my entire staff appeared on this mountain, but I must ask you to promise me one thing: that you will never, ever divulge our secret to anyone.'"

"Are you kidding me?" said Susie, and for a bad minute Megan wondered if the Big Cheese had been right the first time, and her mom might be incapable of keeping such a huge secret. Until she said, "If I told anyone a mouse had been talking to me, they'd lock me up!"

The Big Cheese launched into another series of gestures, as Trey continued his translation. "We are sorry we couldn't tell you before, but we were worried about your propensity to tell the truth at all times. To call a spade a spade. We arranged your job at Camp Green Stars partly for the benefit to the planet, of course, but also to test *your* ability to keep secrets. And our reports have been most reassuring."

"Wait," said Susie. "Wait, wait, wait. Slo-o-o-w down. Slow w-a-a-y down. *You* arranged my job there?"

"Madam," said the Big Cheese, "that's what we do. We arrange things. We manipulate humans. In your case, we persuaded a foundation to set up Camp Green Stars and to employ you to instruct the campers. Of course, the foundation people think they got the idea on their own, without help from anyone, and that it was just by chance that your resume came to their attention."

"I never sent them a resume!"

"Why should you? The one we sent in your name was more than adequate."

Megan's mom was silent for a minute, then she said in a small voice, "And you were *spying* on me there?"

"Of course. How else would we know that you were indeed totally discreet with the secrets of your famous students? That on occasion you even managed to tell 'white lies' to soothe their feelings?"

"I did, didn't I?" said Susie, with a smile. Then she sank back onto the bank with an "Aaargh" sound, her hands over her face.

"Wait a minute," she said. "That note I found on my foot at Green Stars?"

"Mice," said the Big Cheese.

"And that stuff on my bed about where to find Megan?"

"Mice, of course," said the Big Cheese. "And all thanks to one heroic mouse who risked life and limb to give the alarm."

He turned to Savannah, who was still stretched out on Jake's hand. "Talking Mouse Seven, I hereby pronounce you to be Mouse Hero First Class, and I would be delighted if you would do me the honor of riding with me."

"How about that?" said Savannah weakly.

Megan lifted the floppy little body into the cage, where Savannah made her wobbly way to the water bottle and drank deeply before lying down.

There was a skeetering above them on the bluff, and Joey came into sight between the young trees, swinging his way down confidently.

"Yo, Joey!" said his dad. "Meet the fifth Human Who Knows."

"Oh wow," he said.

Megan's mom stood up, smiling, and held out her arms to Joey, who seemed happy to return her hug.

"That's so great," he said. "Fred hoped that was happening.

He sent me to tell you that your movie stars are almost ready."

He noticed the cage, and the patch of mouse under a pink bow.

"Savannah!" he exclaimed. "Is she dead?"

"Not at all," said Trey. "In fact she's so . . . she's so *brave*. She's the one who gave the alarm."

Joey reached in between the bars to tickle Savannah behind the ears, close enough to hear her softly singing: " 'It's a lovely day today. So whatever you've got to do . . .' "

Joey grinned. "This mouse is so . . ." he began, and grinned at Megan, who looked appalled at what dumb joke might come out next. "So-o-o musical."

chapter twenty-seven

his time the Prius could drive up to the main entrance of the lodge to disgorge its four humans and the cage that was now bulging with mice, as Curly, Larry, and Julia had all squashed into it with the Big Cheese and Savannah.

In the big old dining room, everything was ready. The audience was waiting on chairs that had been lined up in three rows. Most of them looked completely starstruck, gazing up at Biff, Nick, Rocky, and Daisy as if they'd never seen humans so perfect, except in the movies. Only Jim-Bob sat in a pose of total surrender.

Uncle Fred looked up from the WATCH computer that would throw the PowerPoint presentation against the wall.

"Almost ready!" he sang out as Megan ran to give him one of those whisper-hugs that the four Humans Who Knew had perfected.

"Mom knows," she whispered.

That prompted Uncle Fred to do one of his slow, elephantine pirouettes, then (because the news was so good) to add an extra one, which was a bit too much for his massive frame and almost spun him into the first row of the audience.

"Clowns!" muttered Jim-Bob, holding up his arms to fend off the gyrating uncle. "Is this how you show respect for us and our opinions?"

"We have plenty of respect for your opinions," said Megan's mom. "You are, of course, entitled to hold any opinion you choose. However, you are not entitled to your own facts, so I beg you to please pay attention to the information that my students are about to give you."

She waved to Rocky to start the presentation, beginning with the agenda:

1. What We Know About Greenhouse Gases (Rocky)
2. The Last Fifty Years (Nick)
3. How Climate Change Will Hurt Animals (Daisy)
4. How We Can Save the Planet (Biff)
5. Questions

And it was awesome.

Megan kept sneaking glances at her mom, who was beaming with pride as her students sliced and diced all the "facts" that the WATCH guys claimed to believe, and replaced them with real ones. They showed how climate change had happened in the past naturally, then made it crystal clear that humans were now warming up their planet much faster than was natural—already causing problems like the torrential rains and fierce storms that tend to happen when the air and the oceans warm up.

Daisy Dakota described how several species of animals were already trying to move to cooler territory, or were going hungry because the changing climate had messed with their food supply.

Then came Biff with his message of hope. That humans can stop the damage, starting right now. And here's how to do it, with new ways of making electricity, and better buildings and cars, and more careful recycling of the planet's resources.

When Biff had finished, it was time for questions.

There was silence. No questions. Susie Miller walked to the front of the room and put her arms around the nearest stars.

"Let's take a vote," she said. "You gentlemen—and ladies—will please decide on a grade for my students here. If you think they were lying to you, if you think they made it all up, give them an F. If they've convinced you that the climate is changing, and that humans are causing it, and we should all do what we can to prevent it, give them an A."

More silence, and Megan noticed that everyone in the audience was looking at Jim-Bob for a lead.

"Would you rather give us the grades in confidence?" asked her mom. "Write them down?"

"There's no need," said Jim-Bob. He looked around at his followers. "They get an A."

"But, boss," said Greasy-hair, "you told us people like these Hollywood pinkos are just out to ruin our country! That's what you said."

"Yeah," said Baldy. "And you told us that *scientists* said all that global warming stuff was garbage."

"Well, maybe they weren't the right sort of scientists," said Jim-Bob.

"You mean, all this time . . . ?" said Baldy.

His voice trailed off. More silence. Then Danny spoke.

"What about the animals, Uncle Jim-Bob?" he asked. "Is it true what she said about those animals?"

"It's true, Danny," said Jim-Bob. "It's all true. It may surprise you to learn," he said, directing his attention to Megan's mom, "I've known the truth for a while now. That your side is right."

"Then why . . . ?" Susie began.

"Why did I keep up with our Web site and all that? I hate to say this, but I did it for the money. And the reason I wanted that information from Savannah here was to get at the big pot of money that's out there. The reward."

"What about us?" asked one of the women. "How will we survive without that money?"

Jim-Bob put his elbows on his knees, and his face in his hands.

"We'll come up with something," he mumbled. "We'll have to."

It was Daisy Dakota who had the idea.

"I've been thinking," she said. "The last couple of days, I've been thinking of ways to maybe get more kids involved. Get *them* working to stop climate change. Hey, Danny?"

She held out an arm toward Danny, and he ran to her.

"Let's you and me start a campaign," she said. "A campaign for the animals."

Megan remembered the task they had set up for the factory workers back in Cleveland.

"Mom, remember that kids' book you wanted to write, on the climate and animals?" she said. "While we've been away, the workers at the factory have been doing some of that research. Sort of as a gift for you."

"The workers?" asked Susie. "*Those* workers?"

But Daisy was off and running. "Great!" she said. "But instead of a book, how about something online, sort of like Facebook? We could call it Creaturebook, and every kid could adopt an animal."

"I love it!" said Megan's mom. "So they'd learn all about their animal, and find out how it's affected by climate change. And their animal could be friends with other animals who have the same problem."

"Whoa!" said Uncle Fred. "Do you know how much computer power that would take? If it gets big?"

Jake laughed. "Sounds like a case for killing two cats with one stone."

"Huh?" said Uncle Fred. Then, "Oh, I get it. Anyone have some computers lying around that aren't doing anything?"

"Are you serious?" asked Jim-Bob, gazing up at him. "We have the computers and the servers, but guys to run them . . . Do they look like computer scientists?"

He waved at his posse of helpers, and it was true that it was easier to imagine them chasing intruders off the mountain than programming computers.

"We can train them," said Jake. He handed Jim-Bob a Planet Mouse business card. "And of course the ladies in your group too. In our business, we know hundreds of computer scientists, so we can set up video courses to help you."

"Please say yes, Uncle Jim-Bob," Danny pleaded. "It would be so cool!"

And so it was agreed: Jim-Bob's group would run Creaturebook off their servers, and if it grew to the point where it needed more servers, they'd buy them and make the extra electricity they needed with solar panels, right here in the valley.

Daisy herself offered some of the start-up money, and the three action heroes agreed to chip in too, but strictly as a loan. They expected Creaturebook to pay for itself quite soon in ads for green products.

For a moment, everybody—Jim-Bob's followers, the five Humans Who Knew, and the four movie stars—just looked at each other. Then Jim-Bob walked over to a computer and wrote out an announcement:

ATTENTION, EVERYBODY!

We are winding up the WATCH organization. Why? Because we no longer believe that climate change is a hoax.

The world's getting hotter, folks, and the evidence is all around us, as all the *real* climate scientists have been saying for years. From now on, my group will devote itself to an on-line project for children called Creaturebook, with our new friend Daisy Dakota.

Watch this site for more details!

"Maybe you could include a picture of Daisy?" suggested Megan's mom. "With an animal?"

It took only a minute for Daisy to go online and download two pictures, one with a super-cute kitten and another with a puppy that was not quite so cute. She was a bit surprised when Megan, Joey, Uncle Fred, and Jake all said it had to be the one with the puppy. Wasn't even close.

chapter twenty-eight

The time came for the humans to split up. The movie stars drove the Jeep back to their camp, with promises that Daisy and a couple of her friends would be back the next day to brainstorm some ideas for Creaturebook.

The five Humans Who Knew squashed into the Prius, dropping Uncle Fred off to follow them in the Mousemobile. They picked up some picnic food in the little town of Irving, then headed up the second valley, the one that hid Camp Green Stars.

Megan's mom knew of a glade beside a creek that was a great place for a picnic. They laid out a blanket where it was shielded by overhead branches from the gaze of hawks so that the six mice who'd been riding in the Prius could come outside without danger.

They were joined by a seventh mouse when Uncle Fred

parked the Mousemobile and brought out Sir Quentin, putting him down beside the others.

"He was severely bent out of shape because he missed all the fun at WATCH," Uncle Fred whispered to Megan. "Though that's not the way he put it. Something about an egregious dearth of esteem for his person."

It so happened that Megan's mom was a huge fan of the English historical dramas that Sir Quentin had watched endlessly at the Talking Academy. Soon, he was deep into memories of favorite episodes. Words like "preternaturally exquisite portrayals" and "ingenious dramaturgy" floated over the picnic site—until Susie's eyes glazed over, and she started looking around for rescue.

And Jake did indeed rescue her, asking her to help him spread out supplies he had brought out of the Mousemobile.

Joey and Megan were tempted by the creek, its water bubbling by, fast and clear. A little way downstream a tree had fallen across, making a precarious bridge.

"Bet you don't dare go across on *that*," said Joey.

"You're on," said Megan, and climbed onto the log. On their side of the creek, the log was broad and dry, but a few feet from the other side the bark had worn off and the log was slippery with spray and moss. Megan ran fast over that section to keep her balance, but lost it anyway, a yard or so from the end, and had to jump onto the far bank. It was quite satisfying to see that when Joey followed, he began to slip even earlier and splashed down in the shallows.

"There must be another way back," he said, tipping water out of his sneakers. He led the way along the bank until they were opposite the picnic site and could watch the others from the high undergrowth.

Megan's mom was at the door of the Mousemobile, peering in, as rows of mice stood at the windows, peering out.

"I'd like to get some plates," she called back over her shoulder to Jake. "But this gas-guzzler of yours is kind of crowded. Maybe they'd all like to come out?"

Jake went over to help, and the watching kids saw him and Megan's mom join their hands in a sort of ladder so the mice could march down, department by department, looking around in amazement at a world few of them had ever seen. And when the last mouse was out, Jake and Susie went on holding hands for a moment or two longer than they needed, whispering something to each other.

Megan looked at Joey and found that he was looking at her as if he had the same thought but wasn't ready to put it into words. He turned and ran farther upstream until he found a place where there were just enough rocks for them to cross, so they could get back to the picnic site in time to shred buns into two thousand pieces, more or less.

It was after the picnic that Megan noticed some urgent-looking activity among the mice. First the Big Cheese conferred with some of his directors. Then he summoned Trey and gave him a message for . . . for her *mom*? Megan actually felt a little jealous as she watched Trey run over to whisper something in her mom's ear, something that made her laugh. Was her *mom* now the most important female on the planet? After knowing about mice for only a couple of hours?

The Big Cheese, it seemed, had thought of a climax for this picnic. Not entertainment. Not a performance by the Youth Chorus. Not a mouse skit or anything else that would fit with this marvelous mood. No, as he now announced, he'd decided to use this moment to finish the legal proceedings of yesterday by pronouncing sentences on the two accused.

Megan caught Trey's eye, and he ran over to her.

"Is he serious?" she whispered.

"Wait," he said. "You'll see."

The Big Cheese climbed onto a small rock where everyone could see him, and Trey rejoined him to translate.

"Today our nation has made excellent progress," he said. "But there is one matter that we must put behind us. Yesterday, we held a trial that found two mice guilty of serious misdeeds—misdeeds that could have led to disaster. Now that the disaster has been averted, I would like to end this chapter in our history—once and for all—by pronouncing the sentences. Director of Forward Planning, please approach."

Looking a bit surprised, a mouse with a red thread around his neck—one with a knot in it—shuffled toward the Big Cheese, a group of guards with toothpicks falling in behind him.

"Mr. Director," said the Big Cheese, "members of the Security Department have been watching you closely and are convinced that you will be, from now on, a loyal member of our nation. I therefore propose to drop all charges against you, because I want to show our human friends how mouse justice works. In our system," he said, turning to face the five humans, "we do not seek revenge. We want only to ensure that our criminals are no longer a threat to our society. And this mouse"—he turned back to the director—"this mouse has been humiliated enough. Indeed, I propose to return him to his old post as Director of Purchasing because I believe that there is no mouse on the planet who will be more careful with our resources."

Megan felt cheated for a moment. Hadn't the director set in motion events that could have brought down his own nation? And now, to let him walk away with barely a slap on the wrist? (If mice have wrists.)

"That wouldn't work for us, unfortunately," whispered her mom. "But for them . . . why not?"

A mouse ran forward to the director, with a red thread in his paws, one with no knot in it, and the director made three pirouettes in a row, throwing off his knotted thread as he did so.

What about Savannah, Megan wondered. Presumably she'd be forgiven too, especially now that she was a hero? But no. It seemed that the Big Cheese had a different sentence in mind. He looked exceptionally stern as he turned to her.

"Talking Mouse Seven," he said. "Approach."

Savannah was not awed. Now that she was strong enough, she even managed a sashay across the picnic blanket on her rear feet.

"You, Mouse," said the Big Cheese, "have already earned the rank of Mouse Hero First Class. But I still intend to sentence you. You will be exiled, forthwith."

Exiled! Being put on a Greyhound bus and sent away as far as that bus would go—it was a punishment that all mice dreaded. Savannah froze, and mouse jaws dropped open. A gasp went up from all the humans except Megan's mom, who was grinning.

The Big Cheese made the "Laughing out loud" sign.

"I sentence you to exile at Camp Green Stars," he said. "You have always worshipped movie stars? Perhaps when you see such stars at close quarters, you will realize that they are no different from other humans. With the approval of Miss Susie, I officially designate you as her mouse companion, to accompany her at all times."

It took a moment for the implication to sink in, but when it did, Savannah rushed up to the Big Cheese to embarrass him with a quick kiss, saying, "Thank you thank you thank you YES!" Then she sprinted over to Megan's mom and jumped on her knee.

"You'll have to promise not to talk to anyone but me, at Green Stars," said Susie, reaching out to tickle Savannah behind an ear. "And not to sing. Ever!"

"Oh, I promise, I promise, I promise," said Savannah. "When

we're with those movie stars I won't say a word. I'll let them think I'm really, really dumb!"

Which almost finished off Trey and Joey and Megan, who rolled off the picnic blanket into a huddle, whispering about the sharpest crayons in the box and the brightest bulbs in the chandelier, until Trey said, "Know what?"

"What?" they asked, seeing that he looked serious now.

"She might not be as dumb as she looks."

And watching Savannah, they had to agree that Trey could be right. From the few words they could hear, she was talking seriously about the climate and how great it was that all those lovely movie stars would help to fix it.

Now all that remained was for all five humans to squash into the Prius and drive up to Camp Green Stars, where the campers poured out of their cabins to greet them, bubbling over with ideas for Daisy's new Web site. Everyone wanted group photographs, and it was Daisy who insisted on getting the photo printed up so all twelve stars could sign copies for Megan and Joey.

And then it was time for Megan and Joey and Jake and Uncle Fred to leave, and to puzzle the stars a bit when they all said fond good-byes to Susie Miller's new mouse, as well as to her.

chapter twenty-nine

t wasn't long before Megan and Joey and Jake were flying over the Rockies on their way to Oregon, speculating about what was going on down there in the two settlements that they could just make out from the plane. Jake pointed out that the track between the two valleys looked quite well worn now, as Jeeps must have gone back and forth with their cargo of movie stars, helping the WATCH guys set up Creaturebook, which would soon be ready to launch. Indeed, the Big Cheese had put together a task force to coordinate it even before the Mousemobile rumbled into Cleveland, and the task force hardly missed a beat as the humans unloaded mice by the boxful, and set them up in the new Headquarters at Planet Mouse.

Headquarters filled three rooms on the second floor of the main house. The humans split up the area with little dividers of balsa wood to give each department its own space, with a larger office for the Big Cheese himself, right next to a small balcony. Uncle Fred drilled a hole in the wall so that for the first time in his life, the Big Cheese could step outside whenever he liked and sniff the air while his muscle mice kept watch for hawks.

And Oregon? Oregon was great. Even greater than Megan had expected, because it began raining brothers.

The first brother came into her life, more or less, when Annie took her up to her old bedroom in the back of the house on Cherry Street. Megan burst out with the surprised reaction she'd been practicing.

"Oh, thank you thank you thank you! You *painted* it for me," she said.

Then she went perhaps the deepest red of her life when Annie said, "I'm so glad you like it, honey, but actually it's for *him*." She patted the belly that had been hiding under a loose shirt but now revealed itself to be quite pregnant.

Which was wonderful, because even though Megan would have to share her dad, she had always wanted a brother or sister. But really, should she have been blindsided by such a big surprise? When she had *mice*?

"We knew," admitted Trey later that day, when Megan had finally managed to get away from Annie with all her excited plans for cribs and names and playpens and even maybe a new house with more room for both kids. "Right, Julia?"

"Of course we knew," said Julia. She'd kept in touch with the mice who had moved into 253 Cherry Street last winter to keep Megan company when all her other mouse friends had gone to Cleveland. "But when humans have secrets from each other—good secrets that won't hurt anybody—we can't tell. It's a mouse rule."

Megan had to admit it had been a good secret, an excellent secret, one that made her dad and Annie exceptionally happy.

And the second brother? Two mice had a hand—a paw—in that. And not just any old mice. Savannah and Julia.

It happened right at the end of a great backpacking trip in the Cascades with Joey and Jake and the four mice, two days before they were due to fly home to Cleveland. They'd almost made it back to the car when Jake saw something that got his attention and he took off down the hill, bounding in great leaps, taking short cuts where the trail switchbacked, leaving the kids gaping at each other.

When they saw Jake again, he was walking slowly back up to meet them with his arm around Megan's mom.

"I was all set to turn east when we closed down the camp," she explained, after she hugged Megan. "Toward Cleveland. Then my friend here—" She reached up and stroked Savannah, who was wearing a cute little sun hat and tiny sunglasses that a famous star had made for her. "My friend here said . . . Oh, you tell them, Savannah. Something about a little bird?"

"Well, it was really a little mouse," said Savannah. She jumped onto Megan's shoulder and pointed at the other shoulder, where Julia was riding. "That little mouse. She e-mailed me about a conversation she'd overheard, soon after you guys got back to Cleveland."

"Oh, no!" said Jake, and actually went a bit pink. "Me and Fred?"

"That's right!" said Savannah. "You and Mr. Fred, talking one night until about two in the morning."

"So what did he say?" asked Joey. "What did my dad say?"

"He said he wanted to marry Susie more than anything in the whole world!" said Savannah, leaping back onto Susie's shoulder. "And I happen to know she wants to marry *him* because that's what I heard her telling a movie star when she thought I wasn't listening!"

Jake went a little dithery, as if he had no clue what to do next.

"Is that true, Dad?" said Joey.

"Yes," he said. "Oh, yes. But only if it's okay with you guys."

Joey and Megan looked at each other, and the silence stretched out a bit as they both came to grips with the notion of being a few steps closer than step-second-cousins.

Megan went first. "Fine with me, bro," she said.

"Me too, sis," said Joey, grinning.

"In fact, it's *great*," said Megan, reaching out to hug both adults at once.

"See?" said Susie to Jake. "It's unanimous, and there's no way you can wriggle out of it now."

There were two ceremonies in Cleveland. First came the boring public one in front of friends from Susie's job, and people who'd known her and Uncle Fred since childhood.

The next day a ceremony took place in the main office of Planet Mouse. Savannah and Julia had been given special permission to wear pink bridesmouse dresses as they rode on Susie's shoulders, under the glow of a thousand solar blobs fastened to fine netting, which transformed the front office of Planet Mouse into a magical bower.

The Big Cheese stood on a pedestal, facing the couple as he intoned in large, slow signs:

"By the authority vested in me by the Mouse Nation, I pronounce you husband and wife."

Then Trey translated the song from the youth chorus:

> Oh, let mice sing and let bells ring.
> We'll all have a mousely fling.
> What a party, what a doozy,
> When our Jake gets wed to Susie.
> It's our nation that began it,
> Making partners for the planet,
> So hear ye, men, and hear ye, mice:
> Married humans—twice as nice.

And afterward, when Jake and Susie had gone off on their honeymoon to the rain forest of Costa Rica? That's when the Big Cheese took steps to repair any damage that the recent closeness to humans might have done to his nation.

In a memo to the Headquarters staff, he wrote:

Lest our proximity to humans should give any
mouse a desire for human comforts, let me

remind you that the events of this past summer, which could have ended tragically, began with such desires. As a reminder of those unfortunate events, I have ordered one doll bed, which will serve as a form of punishment. Mice who appear to be coveting human goods, or aping human ways, will be sentenced to time in bed, so that others may mock them for their pretensions.

The first mouse to undergo punishment by bedtime was a volunteer—the Director of Purchasing. He felt he had not been punished enough and chose to lie in the bed for one whole day while every mouse at Headquarters paraded past, all making the signs for "Laughing out loud." And the foremouse of the factory organized director-viewing field trips for each shift as they came off work.

It was a great reminder, as the Big Cheese told his humans. Attempts to adopt human comforts won't work, and will make you look very silly indeed.